Beyond the Veil: Unraveling the Celestial Tapestry

Earth Energy, Vortices, Portals, Ancient Civilizations and Worship

By

Lisa Lynn

Co-authored by:

God, Angel Nuphriel KGW, and her Divine Team

ISBN: 978-1-963764-29-1 (e-Book)
ISBN: 978-1-963179-67-5 (Paperback)
ISBN: 978-1-963179-68-2 (Hardback)

About the Author

Lisa Lynn is a small-town country farm girl who left the corporate rat race to enjoy a simple, semi-retired farm lifestyle. She is an alternative energy healer using Reiki, crystals, gemstones, and wilderness connections and is an End-of-life Doula.

Lisa has been "sensitive" since a young age, but her ability to channel spirits only started recently. She is being mentored by spirits from the spirit realm and brings forth a very different view of Nikola Tesla's 3 – 6 – 9 observations as it relates to the divine evolution of ancient civilizations, their mastering of earth energy and frequencies, and how the hieroglyphics tell that story.

Through the teachings of one of her mentors, Angel Nuphriel KGW (Angel of mentors), Lisa will show you deciphers that have never been presented before. She will challenge your current views and beliefs of history.

Foreword

I have always had an intuitive sense but was never sure what or how. I could sense things. For example, one time, I had a funny feeling, and then the phone rang, and before the caller could tell me why they were calling – I just blurted it out. There were a few other times I would get tingles when near someone or have dreams where I felt I was awake and in control within the dream.

I had an arsenal of books, though, with a wide range of topics from developing psychic abilities to energy healing, crystal healing, wild medicinal healing and so on. I'm a level 2 Reiki, have gemstone/crystal healing certificates and have used a pendulum for basic yes/no questions, but nothing much more. I've spent a vast amount of my adult life trying to connect with the spirit realm and develop my psychic abilities.

Life had many doors closed and new doors open, with unique and different experiences and alterations to my "Life Plan" along the way.

One of these transitions occurred in 2022-2023. I was in between jobs doing temporary contracts, so I would ask my pendulum yes or no questions about contract extensions or if I should apply for certain positions. I was content with the simple yes or no movements, but also had just started using a mouse pad with Oracle Letters and Numbers. I was still only getting yes or no answers to my questions until one day, there was a really good position that came up that I was very qualified for, but it was full-time, and I was enjoying my current part-time gig, but I asked anyway.

"Should I apply for the job?"

And the pendulum reacted with a no. I was a bit taken aback by the *no* answer, so I just blurted out –"Why not?"

This was the first time I got a spelled-out message, and from there, it was a roller coaster of messages, lessons, and wild goose chases, which I later learned was the spirit realm teaching me how to trust my instincts, how to act instead of reacting to things. This wasn't easy at first, as any book I read or skimmed through certainly did not prepare me for some of the lessons that had me living in fear, crying out of control and my anxiety through the roof or how to differentiate between good or bad spirits. After the fact and reflection, I started to recognize the little signs that were also there, and understanding my gut feelings made it easier to channel. I also burned the mouse pad I was using and reverted to a handmade letter wheel that I could throw out after each use to avoid any spirit attachment.

I had some up-and-down messages and then got a lesson about the proper way to protect myself when opening dialogue. This included how to validate a spirit with lots of questions and, when I felt comfortable, open dialogue. I learned that there are imposture spirits who can be quite convincing, and there are evil ones. Through channeling, I also started to read the bible and found verses that related to the lessons of validation.

1 John: 4, 1 – 6. Believe not every spirit, but "try" the spirits whether they are of God, because many false prophets are gone out into the world.

Matthew 7:15. Beware of false prophets, which come to you in sheep's clothing, but inwardly they are ravening wolves.

I've learned about the spirit realm and the levels and mansions within. The hierarchy that most mediums and psychics are in contact with and the rest that gifted mediums contact. The majority of mediums channel through their guide, who is a go-between to other guides or angels in the spirit realm. I have channeled my ancestral guardian, my birth angel, arch angels, relative and friend spirits, God, and Satan, which is why validation is so important. Although I can feel the conversations in my head, I chose to continue my communications with my pendulum for my own safety, as once the validation process is complete and I open dialogue, spirits have access to your thoughts, and I have the ability to block my own thoughts during dialogue to stop any invasion to the information shared with me by the spirit realm that is not yet meant to be shared. I know that I have been given a rare gift and, with that, a mission. This book is only a piece, a small part of God's mission that I accepted.

***

With the ups and downs I experienced with the learning curve to channeling, my appreciation and greatest thanks go to the love of my life, who somehow, through all these unbelievable communications and interpretations and sometimes sleepless nights, has not once wavered in his belief that there is something tangible here and that it is bigger than either of us could imagine. On days of learning a new glyphic or new history lesson, he would listen intently to the story that unfolded. On nights I would awaken from a bad dream, he would listen and never question the validity of what I was saying. Even channeling his own family members, he took everything in with a smile. With the hypes up and the disappointing downs, he's been my rock.

Contents

Introduction

The information for this writing comes from my divine cosmic team. Each time I take a lesson and reflect, I come to the same realization that only a small fraction of this could possibly be coming from me. They put a bug in my ear, figuratively, and I ran with all the research I could for it. My divine team of spirits, which I have channeled, helped me learn so much in such a small space of time for something that is so far-fetched but makes perfect sense. My divine team has taken me through crash lessons in quantum physics, ancient civilizations, and biblical interpretations and led me to research Tesla's 3 - 6 - 9 theories, Schumann resonances, power of mind, levitation, and the universe in general.

Although some of the channeling will be controversial to some, they are channels that are meant to correct some history and ultimately lead me on my mission as given by my destiny. I am to remind you that we all have a choice, a choice to believe or not to believe, to hear the word given by God and to question known beliefs.

Almost all my guidance and lessons come from various members of my "Divine team." Most of the guidance for research comes from channelings with God or spirit advisors, and the Egyptian hieroglyphic lessons come from a very special friend of mine, who lost his life in a tragic accident. They have played an integral role in writing this book and deserve the title of co-author(s), even though they are not part of this earth realm. To protect the family of my friend, I will refer to his angel name, Angel Nuphriel KGW - Angel of Mentors.

History and even the bible is only an interpretation of events that is someone's word against another. Taken in as myth or fact until another theory comes along that can be scrutinized, disproved, or thrown out by authorities, who perhaps don't want the truth known or proved and adopted. I believe in what I am channeling because the more I see, the more it just makes sense, and there is no other logical explanation for where this information is coming from. I've learned to take a step outside the box, to learn why this information has been kept from other mediums or historians, why only tidbits at a time were given and why I have been privileged to receive this version.

When I first started writing this book, I thought the focus was going to be on the teachings of the Egyptian hieroglyphics. However, the divine communications guided me to various areas to research and encouraged deeper insights into what I was supposed to be looking for. Each divine communication would guide me to research, which all lead down pathways to the universal energetic powers on earth, and to understand this power, looking at ancient civilizations to gain an understanding of how they could have used this power to their advantage. From understanding the relationship between earth frequency and energy and how the ancient civilizations recorded their energy power equations and instructions onto storyboards, and to factor that the positioning of the earth's poles, especially the north pole, has changed over time, and duplication of the energetic resonances are difficult to reproduce on site and impossible to duplicate in a lab.

There are fluctuating earth energy fields all over the world. Some are identified as wonders of the world, others are just recognized as special energy places, like Sedona, and for the commoner like you and I, we are just drawn to places because the energy seems right. Many of these wonders of the world have been studied, and comparisons to astrology, astronomy, and cardinal alignments make assumptions plausible. My divine team has shown me how to find and use a naturally occurring vortex to create natural scaler waves, which is the same method Ancient civilizations found to tap into earth's energy fields by using basic conductors and amplifiers like copper, aluminum, gold, bronze, coal and a variety of crystals and gemstones. This enhanced the power of their bodies and made them capable of absorbing it into their cells, storing, using or transferring it to others through the power of mind using meditation and setting intent.

With each corner taken into research, a whole new thirst for knowledge and a view of the world where ancient mysteries converge with advanced technologies. The patterns point to the existence of a celestial grid that weaves through the fabric of reality and the hidden connections between the ancient landmarks. A grid where the dormant power of the pineal gland unlocks unimaginable mind powers that resonate with the mystical energy networks that connect with cardinal-aligned landmarks across the globe. Each landmark, from Machu Picchu, Easter Island, and Stonehenge to the Egyptian pyramids, plays a crucial role in maintaining balance and harmony in the universe, all of which ties back into the Creation of mankind itself intertwined with Greek mythology and the teachings within the bible.

There exists an interconnection between a fully awakened pineal gland, the celestial grid, ancient civilizations and the divine. Through my channeling with the divine team, God says it is time to reveal truths, not half-truths or bits and pieces that have been released throughout the years. It's time to challenge science and open to the possibilities of what is being revealed about ancient civilizations and the ethereal connections between them. These connections include:

1. Ancient Alien Influences:

Ancient artifacts and inscriptions that hint at extraterrestrial guidance in the construction of the landmarks. There are hidden messages and drawings left by these beings, revealing a purpose beyond human understanding. Hidden chambers and secrets within the landmarks containing advanced ancient technologies and how they can be harnessed to restore balance to the celestial grid.

2. Quantum Energy Fields and Energy Manipulation:

Landmarks are used as quantum nodes, resonating with a universal energy field. The earth's frequency and resonance with atmospheric energies synchronized with the celestial grid and those with awakened pineal powers that can extend to telekinesis and the manipulation of energy and shape reality or influence the environment.

3. Celestial Connections:

Celestial events are key triggers for activating or enhancing the grid. Cosmic alignment is the focal point to harness the celestial energies. People with an awakened pineal gland resonate with specific celestial events, aligning their powers with the rhythm of the universe. These alignments amplify their abilities and unlock new facets of the celestial grid.

4. Interdimensional Gateways:

Ancient rituals and technologies that can activate the landmarks as interdimensional gateways. Uncover the true definition of realms, dimensions, and universes that can unlock these gateways, encountering alternate realities and unlocking the mysteries of existence. An awakened pineal gland can view into these realms, dimensions, and universe, but with that, comes danger and death.

5. Living Earth Consciousness:

Commune with the earth's consciousness through meditation and ancient practices and connect with the sentient spirit of the planet, learning about its history, desires, and the imminent threat to its well-being. With awakened pineal powers, the ability to enter shared mindscapes, where thoughts and memories intertwine. Telepathy becomes a means of communication within the group, allowing the sharing of knowledge.

6.   Vortex Energy and Portals:

Time resonance to navigate temporal anomalies and quantum leap between activated portals to view ruins or civilizations around the world that are connected to the celestial grid. The awakened pineal gland unlocks gateways to alternate dimensions.

7.   Biblical Relationships

Celestial relationship with 3 – 6 – 9, and the worship of God, the universe, and Satan. The relationship between the first Olympian Gods and archangels and the wars for freedom of choice.

Why now? The triad between God, Satan, and the universe needs to be better understood. There is a cosmic battle coming where the fate of the world hangs in the balance. The revelation about a new era of understanding, where humanity and the cosmos are forever changed. One that we have been waiting for since the death of Christ and the anticipated arrival of the second coming.

To venture forward in this book, you need to leave what we know of science behind and open your mind to all the connections and possibilities my divine team has led me to discover. Pieces of historical discoveries through Greek philosophers, Einstein, Nikola Tesla, archaeologists, astronomers, historians, ancient astrologers, and other mediums around the world that have theories that interconnect.

3 – 6 – 9 Illustration

It's difficult to define how far back to look to find when relationships between energy and frequencies were first recorded. We can determine a historical account of astronomy, philosophy, mathematics, and geography as an example of recorded history prior to the birth of Christ. Some of the most notable are worth mentioning below. A complete list can be found on Wikipedia.

- Anaxagoras (500 – 428 BC) Pre-Socrates Greek philosopher introduction of Nous (intellect or intelligence (human mind)
- Socrates (470 – 399 BC) Greek philosopher
- Plato (428 – 424 BC)
- Aristotle (384 – 322 BC) Ancient Greek philosopher, metaphysics, mathematical logic
- Strato of Lampsacus (335 – 269 BC), philosopher of natural science
- Aristarchus of Samos (310 – 230 BC) Greek astronomer, mathematician
- Hipparchus (190 – 120 BC) Greek astronomer, geographer, and mathematician – founder of trigonometry and discovery of the equinoxes

And in current times:

- Nicolaus Copernicus (1473 – 1543) – notable for studies placing the sun as the center of the universe rather than earth.
- Isaac Newton (1642 – 1726) – Laws of Motion and universal gravitation
- Johannes Kepler (1571 – 1630) – Kepler's law of Planetary Motion
- Albert Einstein (1879 – 1955) – Theory of Relativity
- Winfried Otto Schumann (1888 – 1974) – Schumann resonances
- Nikola Tesla (1856 – 1943) – Wireless energy – theory of 3 – 6 – 9

The context for earth power is based on theories and studies from the later 6. More so with the Schumann resonances and Nikola Tesla's wireless free energy and fascination with 3 – 6 – 9.

The wireless free energy concept utilizes the earth's energy frequency and atmospheric energy to create an electrical system of endless power. Although his concentration was on electricity or wireless electricity, his discoveries were also based on geometry and vortex mathematics, which involves polygon geometry. Nikola Tesla is alleged to have stated, "If you only knew the magnificence of the 3 – 6 – 9 , then you would have the key to the universe." The 3 – 6 – 9 phenomena have been theorized and applied to the universal laws of attraction and the laws of manifestation and have made their way into mainstream social media, but do people really understand the principles and God's depiction behind the numbers?

To understand the mathematics behind 3 – 6 – 9, we need to be familiar with how every number and mathematical equation product can be reduced to the primary numbers between 1 – 9, which is referred to as the digital root. Simplified, if we look at the power of two, where the sum number is doubled, and so on, a digital root pattern emerges. We use the power of two, as it demonstrates the beginning of life, where one cell is divided into 2 and then doubles and doubles again until the cumulative cells begin to create a DNA structure of organic matter. The illustrations below represent how we derive the digital root patterns based on the basic power of two or other variations. The key is in the digital root, the relationship with divinity and worship, and the relationship that connects to the existence of intelligent life on earth.

Basic Power of 2			
Number	Sum Product		Digital Root
1			1
2			2
4			4
8			8
16	1 + 6 = 7		7
32	3 + 2 = 5		5
64	6 + 4 = 10	1 + 0 = 1	1
128	1 + 2 + 8 = 11	1 + 1 = 2	2
256	2 + 5 + 6 = 13	1 + 3 = 4	4
512	5 + 1 + 2 = 8		8
1024	1 + 0 + 2 + 4 = 7		7
2048	2 + 0 + 4 + 8 = 14	1 + 4 = 5	5
4096	4 + 0 + 9 + 6 = 19	1 + 9 = 10 1 + 0 = 1	1
8192	8 + 1 + 9 + 2 = 20	2 + 0 = 2	2

The Same Pattern Arises Even If We Use Half Numbers			
Number	Sum Product		Digital Root
1			1
0.5			5
0.25	2 + 5 = 7		7
0.125	1 + 2 + 5 = 8		8
0.0625	6 + 2 + 5 = 13	1 + 3 = 4	4
0.03125	3 + 1 + 2 + 5 = 11	1 + 1 = 2	2
0.015625	1 + 5 + 6 + 2 + 5 = 19	1 + 9 = 10 1 + 0 = 1	1
0.0078125	7 + 8 + 1 + 2 + 5 = 23	2 + 3 = 5	5
0.00390625	3 + 9 + 6 + 2 + 5 = 25	2 + 5 = 7	7
0.001953125	1 + 9 + 5 + 3 + 1 + 2 + 5 = 26	2 + 6 = 8	8
0.0009765625	9 + 7 + 6 + 5 + 6 + 2 + 5 = 40	4 + 0 = 4	4
.00048828125	4 + 8 + 8 + 2 + 8 + 1 + 2 + 5 = 38	3 + 8 = 11	2

In the first figure, a pattern repeats itself and starts to emerge.

1 2 4 8 7 5

You might say that's because we are doubling, but there are odd numbers in this sequence, and 3 – 6 – 9 is missing.

In the second figure, it's a similar pattern, except the sequence of the numbers has changed.

1 5 7 8 4 2

The 3 – 6 – 9 are missing.

The pattern or sequence of the numbers comes into play when the geometrical pattern or vortex math forms shape, also referred to as Sacred Geometry.

Sacred Geometry is the study of the spiritual meaning of various shapes. It can be applied to the forms, numbers, and patterns seen throughout the natural world. A snowflake, the spiral of a snail's shell, and the branches of a tree can all be connected to examples of Sacred Geometry. The basic and simplest diagram for Scared Geometry is the digital root polygon. Starting with a circle, and the even spacing of 1 to 9 and using the sequence of digital root for the basic power of two. When you join the numbers in order 1 2 4 8 7 5 or 1

5 7 8 4 2 – you arrive at the same polygon shapes. And then when 3 – 6 – 9 is joined, an equilateral triangle emerges.

Figure on the left. It does not matter which number you start at *1 2 4 8 7 5* or *1 5 7 8 4 2*, you derive the same pattern.

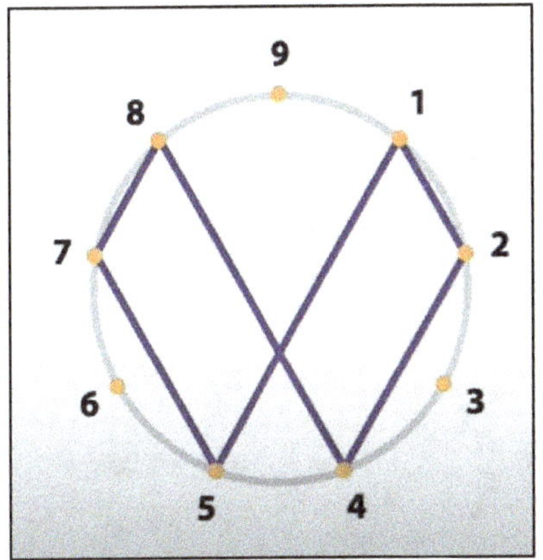 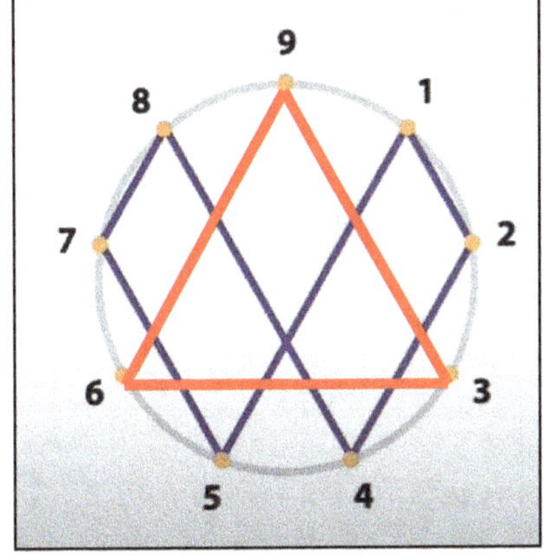

On the right, when we join 3 – 6 – 9, we see another pattern equilateral triangle.

All angles 60°: 60 + 60 + 60 = 180 1 + 8 = 9

3 + 6 + 9 = 18   1 + 8 = 9

When we look at the basic doubling principle for 3 – 6 – 9, similar patterns start to emerge. Starting at 3, each digital root result is either 3 or 6, but 9 is not in this sequence. When 9 is used in basic doubling, the digital root result will always be 9.

Looking at 3 – 6 – 9 specifically, the similar pattern appears.

```
3
6
12      1 + 2 = 3
24      2 + 4 = 6
48      4 + 8 =12        1 + 2 = 3
96      9 + 6 = 15       1 + 5 = 6
192     1 + 9 + 2 = 12   1 + 2 = 3
384     3 + 8 + 4 = 15   1 + 5 = 6
768     7 + 6 + 8 = 21   2 + 1 = 3
```

The sequence of 9 will always be the digital route of 9.

```
9
18      1 + 8 = 9
36      3 + 6 = 9
72      7 + 2 = 9
144     1 + 4 + 4 = 9
288     2 + 8 + 8 = 18     1 + 8 = 9
```

Other areas where digital root can be applied is with solfeggio healing frequencies in relation to Chakra and Sanskrit meditation chanting and the basic tuning fork resonances.

The Solfeggio	Chakra (Mantra) Frequencies	Digital Root
852 – Third Eye	(Ohm) (Love frequency)	8+5+2=15 1+5=6
528 – Solar Plexus	(Ram) (Positive transformation)	5+2+8=15 1+5=6
963 – Crown	(Ohm) (feeling one with mind)	9+6+3=18 1+8=9
369 – Root	(Lam) (Unconscious blockages)	3+6+9=18 1+8=9
639 – Heart	(Yam) (Harmonize relationships)	6+3+9=18 1+8=9
741 – Throat	(Ham) (Remove toxins)	7+4+1=12 1+2=3
417 – Sacral	(Vam) (Remove negative energy)	4+1+7=12 1+2=3

$$
\begin{array}{llll}
\multicolumn{4}{c}{\text{Tuning fork frequencies related to healing.}} \\
\multicolumn{4}{c}{\text{A standard set of 3 tuning forks for healing contains:}} \\
\end{array}
$$

Tuning fork frequencies related to healing.
A standard set of 3 tuning forks for healing contains:

128	$1 + 2 + 8 = 11$	$1 + 1 = 2$
256	$2 + 5 + 6 = 13$	$1 + 3 = 4$
512	$5 + 1 + 2 = 8$	

Or

4096	$4 + 9 + 6 = 19$	$1 + 9 = 10$	$1 + 0 = 1$
4160	$4 + 1 + 6 = 11$	$1 + 1 = 2$	
4225	$4 + 2 + 2 + 5 = 13$	$1 + 3 = 4$	

Recognize the patterns: 2 4 8 1

Except 5 and 7 are missing.

I mention Sanskrit and sound frequencies because people believe that the higher frequency level is what determines healing or enlightenment. Others connect $3 - 6 - 9$ in other spiritual ways, for example:

1. Manifestation

$3 - 6 - 9$ is a method that involves writing down your desired manifestation three times in the morning, six times during the day, and nine times in the evening. This repetition throughout the day is believed to reinforce your intention and signal the universe to bring your desire into reality. 3 is usually the primary to set intent.

2. Ancient Civilizations

Pyramids are built in almost a perfect equilateral triangle, which demonstrates 3 – 6 – 9.

3. Mathematics

3 – 6 – 9 is used in a variety of formulas and equations, including number theory and geometry. In geometry, the number 3 – 6 – 9 is used to represent the Pythagorean Theorem, which is one of the most important concepts in geometry.

4. Technology

Nikola Tesla was known for his groundbreaking work in the field of electromagnetism. He developed electrical circuits and energy systems based on the principles behind 3 – 6 – 9.

5. Spirituality and Philosophy

3 – 6 – 9 is associated with enlightenment and spiritual awakening. Many ancient cultures believed that these numbers represented the divine principles of Creation and the universe and used them as a symbol of spiritual power.

3 – 6 – 9, with the relationship to cardinal alignments and awakened pineal glands, opens the possibilities that will defy science.

The Divine Relationship With 3 – 6 – 9

The information about the divine relationship of 3 – 6 – 9 is channeled through my divine team in the spirit realm.

There is a relationship between Nikola Tesla's 3 – 6 – 9 fascination that is associated with sacred geometry and the universe itself. The universe is designed of smaller particles that can be manipulated by thought and energy. With Tesla's theory, the digital root of a number played importance, with the 3 – 6 – 9 being the most influential. For example, the energy created by earth is 7.83hz and is relative to the universe by its energy emitted 432hz. The digital root of each $7 + 8 + 3 = 18$ $1 + 8 = 9$ or $4 + 3 + 2 = 9$

As seen with the digital root calculations, 9 stands out. That is because "9" IS the "God Frequency", or representation of our universe and life itself. Nine months to give birth, there are 9 realms, 9 mansions, and 9 dimensions to earth and 6 universes that exist together. Each realm, dimension or universe has a purpose and a color associated with it.

These teachings come from conversations with God.

Realms

- Realm 1 – Greenish Brown – Is earth, the human realm – where we currently exist
- Realm 2 – Yellowish Orange – Is space – where the universe is
- Realm 3 – Whiteish Blue - is UFO – alien realm
- Realm 4 – Blueish purple – Is the mystical creature realm
- Realm 5 –Orange – Is Satan's realm
- Realm 6 – White – Is the purgatory realm
- Realm 7 – White – Is the spirit realm
- Realm 8 – Gold – Angels realm
- Realm 9 – Gold – Arch Angels and God realm

Mansions

Mansions are different levels of learning a soul goes to within the "Heaven realms 6 - 9.

- Mansion 1 - is for rotten behavior. Someone who misbehaves all the time or for bullying
- Mansion 2 - is for those who were mean to people or hurt people

- Mansion 3 - is for your own forgiveness or forgiveness you give to others

- Mansion 4 - is for those who need to work on their mistakes, when they didn't follow their life plan

- Mansion 6-is for people who need to be forgiven for their sins

- Mansion 7 -is where you make amends with yourself

Purgatory - is where a soul who has done really bad things or won't take accountability for their actions go. It's like solitary confinement. They do not interact with other souls, and they are not allowed to contact souls in other mansions or the earth plane. God may allow them to contact a medium to make a plea for forgiveness. If a medium is claiming to speak with a soul from here, they likely are NOT, and only getting messages from the souls' guardian, birth angel or arch angel.

8-9 Represents the Angel and God mansions.

Dimensions

- Dimension 1 – Main – where we are now

- Dimension 2 – Time – Timeline of the lives we are living

- Dimension 3 – Place – Physical locations of where we are
- Dimension 4 - Death – Where we (the soul) go to prepare for the body to die
- Dimension 5 – Satan
- Dimension 6 – Absolution
- Dimension 7 – Energy
- Dimension 8 – Forgiveness
- Dimension 9 – Eternal Life

Each dimension exists simultaneously at the same time and corresponds with the 9 realms.

Universes

- Universe 1 – Solar system
- Universe 2 – Milky Way
- Universe 3 – Mini universe (where science makes sense)
- Universe 4 – Universal law
- Universe 5 – Time (Biological clock)
- Universe 6 – Main universe

Each universe carries a part of your spirit energy. Thus, the analogy that we exist in multiple universes.

We primarily exist in the Mini-universe, Solar System, and the Milky Way, which overlap each other to give the illusion it's one. People only understand what they see and what they are told by scientists, who again also study only what they can see.

The universe has black holes, which are portals to other galaxies. Science is afraid of the unknown, where the reliance is on what they see or can verify by tested hypothesis.

The law of relativity states everything is neutral. Everything is relative. It is we who attach meaning and emotions to each event and experience we encounter in life. Black holes are the key to other galaxies' solar systems with planets with civilizations like earth. If we were to send a ship through a black hole, they would see other solar systems. It could see and record and could come back with information if programmed to return. There are other universes like ours and multiple solar systems in one universe.

Nikola Tesla was so close to realizing this divine connection, except his focus was on the power capabilities and later weapons of destruction. Even the Schumann resonances were on to something that science got in the way of taking it further.

In the previous chapter, we looked at the basic power of 2, which gave a digital root sequence of 1 2 4 8 7 5 or when reduced by half doubled 1 5 7 8 4 2. Solfeggio, Chakra, or Sanskrit showed digital root sequences of 3 6 and 9, and tuning fork frequencies missing 5 and 7. What is the relationship of these digital root numbers with universal and Creation?

By God's definition - 3 – 6 – 9 signifies the beginning, middle, and end.

The first intelligent population of earth were the terrestrial aliens (Dimension 3). They came to this universe and to this planet as their own solar system was dying. They represent the beginning as the aliens were essentially responsible for transporting other species to this and other planets as a method of protecting and ensuring the survival of energy beings (people, plants, animals, etc.). Introducing species also meant the introduction of laws, which then created consequences that lead to redemption, which leads to punishment (Dimension 6), which leads to the forgiveness of sin, which leads to justice (Dimension 9), which leads to the

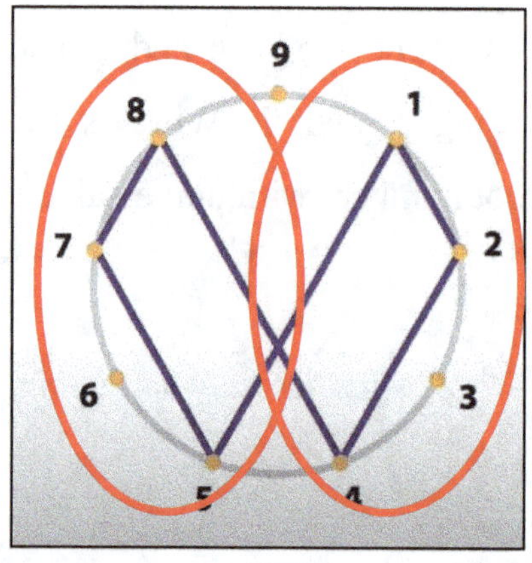

Looking back at the polygon of
the basic digital root 1 – 9. Nine stands alone at the top
(God), 5, 6, 7, 8 represent divinity, 1, 2, 3, 4 represent all
life. It has a resemblance to a scale. The "Karmic Scale of
Justice."

9 (God's realm) controls both sides. The left is Heaven and
Satan, and the right is Creation (life of beings).

The divine relationship in the polygon also connects to the
significance of the cardinal alignments. north, south, east,
and west are also representations of the divine significance

of 3 – 6 – 9, where the north represents God, the south represents Satan, and the universe is represented by the Milky Way. The east-west connection is Equinox (the rising and setting of the sun and moon). Beginning and End. The constellation and the stars factor in with seasons, astronomy, astrology, and navigation.

Earth also represents the divine scales, where the celestial grid (central alignment with the center of the earth) coincides with the ancient landmarks. The Great Pyramid is aligned with Machu Picchu, the Nazca lines and Easter Island along a straight line around the center of the earth, within a margin of error of less than one-tenth of one degree of latitude. Just as every point along the equator is 6,215 miles from both the north and south poles, every point along the line of ancient sites is 6,215 miles from two axis points on earth.

We have looked at all the digital root numbers except 5. By God's definition, 5 represents the realm and dimension where Satan is. If the north is God, the south is Satan, and the celestial grid is in the middle, then the celestial grid represents the free choice to worship one or the other or both.

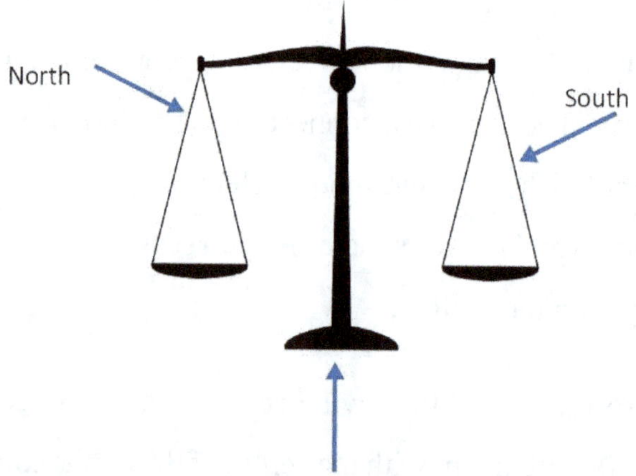

The Celestial line of balance that align ancient landmarks

Balance represents free choice, or free will and balance between good and bad. The Universal Law is about balance. Karma, if you may.

The celestial grid is where north and south power meet and the energy at that intersection is so important to the alignment of ancient civilizations.

It's interesting that in the healing frequencies, the digital root 5 is not there. Why would healing be related to Satan in the 5th realm and 5th dimension, but it appears with the other sequences, further enforcing the balance and will of choice?

To make sense of this, we need to go way back to the earliest of times when Cronos (Satan) originally sat with God in the spirit realm. He might have been a bit rebellious at times, but it was when Satan became greedy and wanted to rule earth and its inhabitants himself. Scripture's Luke 10:18 and Matthew 25:41 make references to Satan falling from heaven or Satan and his angels who will be thrown into hell.

We look to the beginning of time when ancient Greek mythology began when the gods were referred to as Primordial Gods. Although there may be a slight misrepresentation of the genealogy (father, son, cousins) of the gods, the War of the Titans represents the first war between God, Satan (Cronos), and the other earthly gods.

To end this war, one of the gods gave up his immortal life as a sacrifice to maintain the will of choice and maintain balance in the universe, resulting in the banishing of Satan from the spirit realm to the 5th realm and 5th dimension, sending mystical creatures to the 4th realm, and returning the Olympian Gods who survived the war to the spirit realm 9 as the Arch Angels that we know of today. The world is not ready to know who is who in terms of Gods to archangels.

The next war between Satan and God is documented in the bible, where God sent Jesus.

What is not written is how the war between the people was also connected to the fight for a universal law, one of which there is only 1 law. Sounds great until you break down what

1 law represents. It means there is no longer a choice. Consequences and punishment are one and the same, which is the end of life. There is no redemption, no forgiveness, no room for justice or karmic correction. In simple terms, this means that if you break the law, your energetic soul does not get a chance to be reborn. It ends. Satan represents the end of energetic soul life; he feeds on it. Current bible and religion cite that Jesus died for our sins, but he also sacrificed himself for mankind to continue having choices. To continue to have the ability to redeem oneself, to get forgiveness and then to be reborn to justify and balance the soul's karmic purpose.

Scripture says there will be a second coming of Christ, whether born male or female. The war between Satan and God is brought upon by the people whom they worship and follow. There is a term of time until Satan's return, and as we approach the term, Satan is already building up his army. But it is not an army of demons or dead spirits. It is the souls who walk the earth who have taken sides with Satan, whether by intent or those who unknowingly signed a devil contract. These contract souls, when dead, will vanish. They do not get to be reborn.

How can you sign a contract without knowing?

Mathew 7:15: "Beware of the false prophets, which come to you in sheep's clothing, but inwardly they are ravening wolves."

There is a lot of hype these days, thanks to social media, about the law of attraction, the law of manifestation, third eye or pineal gland activation, and Solfeggio frequencies that promise results, but the results are few and usually selfishly driven. Greed and Selfishness are not in the universe to reward upon. Greed and Selfishness are reaped by Satan's thirst and hunger for souls. Look at the frequency digital root of things you are listening to – if it is 5, beware. If you think the 5th dimension is the God frequency, or the higher self, think again.

When the list of mansions were provided by the divine team, I didn't notice at first that they left out Mansion 5. It wasn't until the first drafts of this book were done that I caught that, so I asked the divine team about mansion 5.

Mansion 5 - is Hell, where souls do not like or believe in God and still want to follow Satan. Satan lets them come here for torture and to be spies.

I'm not sure about anyone else, but I am starting to believe that the mark of the beast is 5 5 5, not 6 6 6 as we have all been led to believe to this point.

It's not just social media. How many times do people fall into despair, sorrow, grief, depression, fear, and disease and beg for a way to release the pain or want something so bad that they say to themselves, "I'll do anything"? That is a calling or opening the door to welcome Satan to your soul. Picture this: you worship God, you lead a good life with little sin, and you anticipate that going to Satan's realm is not in your cards, but when the war begins and the contracts are called – you have no choice but to be in his army – and when you die – there is no coming back in another life.

Let this be a lesson or warning: the 5th dimension and 5th realm lead to Satan.

With reference to reaching a higher state of being, awakening the pineal gland, the first intelligent species on earth came with awakened pineal glands. Civilizations like Atlantis and the higher rulers in Ancient Egypt and other ancient civilizations. God controls what can or can not be activated in the pineal gland, and God controls what can be manifested from the universe. A fully activated pineal gland opens the brain to the universe, everything that the 9 dimensions and realms represent. The pineal gland is there for the divine protection of people. At best, social media claims to awaken the pineal gland by opening the third eye, and some mediums or spiritual people may tap into 1 or 2 of the realms, but not all.

For people on the bandwagon of activating the pineal gland, look at the 9 dimensions and realms. In realms 3 and 4, UFOs and mystical creatures do not want to interact with people, and any purposeful contact on the human part would likely lead to death. Most people are not strong enough to withstand Satan in realm or dimension 5. With a fully awakened pineal gland, any entity from these realms or dimensions can come to you in the earth plane, so be thankful that God is protecting you from full pineal activation.

As a side note, the portals to realms 3 and 4 protect and hide those creatures, although they visit the earth plane often. I would be sure that with every "bigfoot" sitting, a vortex with a portal is in the area. People report seeing UFOs emerge and disappear into thin air.

Look at a different perspective: when we are born, we are born of pure spirit. Born with the knowledge carried in the heavenly realms, which is basically everything. A baby can't communicate, and through the process of "conditioning," it is taught that we do not see things that adults can't explain. Children eventually lose their ability to see and connect with the spirit realms. A young child learning to color will choose green, blue, red, yellow, orange, or purple to color people or animals, and parents or teachers correct them. When they are young, they are still connected and can see the spirit realm, where they have access to the Book of Life, and they would see things in the vibrant colors of our chakras or aura. It's with that conditioning that we tell children people are not green or blue, that the pineal gland starts to close to protect the brain as connections are made to the seen or perceived reality around them referred to as "science."

Pineal Gland, Earth Energy, Universal Power

A simple Google search of the power of the mind returns a massive list of articles and books, so why is it so hard for people to believe that ancient civilizations, and our current one, could use the power of their minds, combined with the endless electromagnetic energy generated from the earth and atmosphere.

We already see in historical artifacts that the intelligence level of Atlanteans, Aztecs, Egyptians, et cetera was far superior and advanced than our current day scientists can understand, even though in current times, breakthroughs are being discovered in the use of meditation and frequency for healing and DNA repairing. Our bodies create a low voltage current at rest, and in concentrated tests of activity, 100 – 2000 watts of power output have been measured. We also know that levitation is possible through deep states of meditation, and science can recreate anti-gravity situations using electric machines.

Consider the story of Coral Castle. Huge blocks of coral or other stone weighing between 9 – 25 tonnes each would be delivered, with the instruction to leave the trailer overnight to be unloaded. Neighbors reported that no machinery was heard, yet in the morning, when the trucks came back for their trailers, they were indeed unloaded and stones placed with precision.

Whenever Edward Leedskainin was asked about how he moved the blocks, he would only reply that he understood the laws of weight and leverage well and that he had discovered the secrets of the pyramids. After Edward Leedskainin died in 1951, they discovered a series of circuits underground and noted a box placed on top of his leverage device that is guessed to have created an anti-gravity field, which is how a man with a stature of 5'1" could achieve such an astonishing feat.

The frequency of earth is 7.83hz, and the universe is 432hz as measured today. Earth itself grows at a rate of approximately 40,000 tons of material each year and loses about 95,000 tons of hydrogen gases from earth's atmosphere into outer space. Simple mathematics would suggest that the earth was smaller thousands or 100,000 thousand years ago when the giants and ancient civilizations were at their peak. This also means that the earth's gravitational Force would have been less, making it easier to levitate and move objects. Tapping into heightened earth frequencies and amplifying these frequencies in combination with the human organic makeup of particles to cells to tissue to organs/bones to the body is all related to energy. In general, in mechanical or physics terminology – energy is used to create power, that creates motion, etc.

The simple act of walking, for example. Uses energy stored in the body to move your legs to and fro, to create movement. The friction from each step to the surface creates momentum, which creates movement. You exert more bodily energy that makes you walk faster or run. Energy, momentum, velocity, acceleration, distance, et cetera.

Looking at human energy or the power of the mind specifically, and the known aspects of energy other than motion. Every part of the body vibrates at its own rhythm, and the brain is no exception with its own unique brainwaves and frequency. In neuroscience, there are five distinct brainwave frequencies, namely the Beta Waves, Alpha Waves, Theta Waves, Delta Waves, and the lesser-known Gamma Waves. Each brainwave frequency, measured in cycles per second (Hz), has its own set of characteristics representing a specific level of brain activity and a unique corresponding state of consciousness.

Beta waves (12-30Hz) are present in normal waking consciousness and are heightened during times of stress. Alpha waves (7.5-14Hz) are those of deep relaxation and visualization and are the first frequency for meditation. Theta waves (4-7.5Hz) are present in deep meditation and light sleep. The slowest Delta brainwave frequency (0.5-4Hz) is that of deep, dreamless sleep and transcendental meditation. The less recognised Gamma brainwaves are the fastest at above 40Hz and are associated with sudden insight.

The optimal brainwave frequency for visualization and meditation is the Alpha-Theta border at 7-8Hz. It opens the gateway to your subconscious mind and, hence, to consciously impress the universal mind with your desires. At this frequency of brainwaves, you can intentionally create your reality through the power of your imagination. Note that the average range for alpha-theta is between 4 and 14hz, which is right where the universal frequency 9 fits in.

The internet is full of different opinions and research, but I was drawn to this website https://www.mind-your-reality.com/thought_power.html and three articles in particular: Brainwaves and Consciousness, Thought Power and the One Universal Mind. Specifically, the energy relationships between frequencies and thought. And when I think of the power of the mind, three aspects come to mind. Telepathy, Telekinesis, and Remote Viewing.

Telepathy is the ability to transmit thoughts or information from one person's mind to another. Remote viewing is the ability to perceive or acquire information and imagery of distant or remote geographical targets. Both are associated with extrasensory perception (ESP) and associated with the ability to go deep within your mind beyond all "five" senses through meditative practices. Telekinesis is the hypothetical ability allowing an individual to influence a physical system without physical interaction.

In addition to the aspect of the power of the mind, each human cell and the composition of each to our body form producing energy, but here is where traditional science conflicts with universal science, as electricity, in the sense of electrical current, is not the same as universal energy, even though the universal energy can translate into volts, amps and watts. An excess of electrical energy can kill a person, whereas an excess of universal energy in the organic body is like a supercharged human, but there are limitations as well.

Each human cell is capable of producing approximately 1.4 volts of electricity. Although this may not sound like a lot, when multiplied by the 38 trillion cells in our body, we arrive at an astonishing 55 trillion volts or the equivalent of 55 billion lightning bolts! And a human cell generates 0.07 volts of electricity. That means a human body with 37.5 trillion cells can theoretically produce 2.625 trillion volts of electricity. That's enough to power a small country or fry an elephant.

There is scientific bias and proof about energy and the human capability to harness such energy and use it with either the power of the mind or superhuman strength. Yet, when we look at ancient civilizations, science wants to rule out this energy as a plausible means by which pyramids or other monolithic sites were constructed. It's through the wonders of the world that the power of the earth is revealed.

The most controversial use of earth power with human power of mind is around the history of ancient Egypt. Historians claim that the tombs and sarcophagi of pharaohs, together with hieroglyphics, represent royalty, but what is not implied is the symbols of power or elements used to absorb, use, transfer or store earth and body energy (voltage).

Energy power in the Egyptian era was much more than that of a Pharaoh and his queens. Ancient Egyptians perfected the power of mind, the power of earth's energy frequency combined with metals, crystals, and natural resources. They perfected the basic earth battery to defy gravity to levitate and move heavy objects. They perfected the first glimpse of setting intentions with vision boards to God's universe and the Universal Laws of Attraction and Manifestation. This is not just another theory of the meanings of hieroglyphics but an actual formula that could be proved by scientists out in the field, considering natural earth energy is not something that can be recreated to perfection in a lab.

Egyptians understood the power between elements, frequency and energy. When we look at the composition of the human body in relation to the percentage of water and the capacity to hold energy and the 37.2 trillion cells within the body that each hold 60% water, we can see a powerhouse. When we say 60% cell and 60% body for a combined 120 earth power times 32 trillion (average of male at @ 36 trillion and female 28 million (36+28)/2=32). 120 (static watts) divided by 32 trillion, which results in 3.75e-12 (0.00000000000375). (Clarification – 1 cell can absorb 120 earth amps of power) An electricity amp is not the same as an earth energy amp.

Earth's frequency is measured as 7.83hz, which equals 10 earth amps. 7.83hz = 10 earth amps (ea) = 2000 ohms and if the average human resonates with 60hz = 76.6283 earth amps.

When frequencies are combined, a beat is created until a common resonance occurs and the frequency steadies. For example, a frequency of 100 and 109 – will reduce the difference, which in this example is 9.

In another perspective, a tuning fork is at 4096hz, and another is at 4225hz (4225-4096=129). (1+ 2 + 9 = 12) (1 + 2 = 3) If we combine those sound frequencies with earth's (7.83 – 3 = 4.83), which sets a frequency or vibration with natural energy (not artificially produced) which falls in the range of alpha-theta which represents healing and much more.

Earth has a unique electromagnetic signature that resonates between the north and south poles. Earth is also known to have energy anomalies, where higher concentrations of energy are felt. It's known that pyramids, especially those in the northern hemisphere, have openings to the north. They are also an exact equilateral triangle (3 – 6 – 9). It's also known that the pyramids and other wonders of the world emit a higher-than-normal energy that is almost calming, peaceful or healing and were likely built on vortex-like anomaly spots. However, over time, as the earth's surface has grown, gravitational pulls change, and the earth wobbles. The poles have changed, and in places like Stonehenge, the shift in polar alignment has made a significant change in the power amplification of vortex energy.

Antiquity Reborn, Mario Buildreps, https://www.mariobuildreps.com/ has done amazing research on the polar alignments and details the north pole shifts and alignments, and his research is worth exploring.

Energy. Everything is made and resonates around energy. With every equation, we look at what we know to determine or find the missing link. In this case, we are looking at earth frequencies and earth energy and their relationships. We are looking at Einstein's Theory of Relativity, quantum physics, quantum magnetic pulses, kinetics, kinematics, cymatics, amps, watts, Tesla 3 – 6 – 9, Schumann's resonances, grounding, and basic elements used as amplifiers. We are looking at how to defy gravity, as Edward Leedskainin did at Coral Castle. And with the Egyptian civilizations, the story has been in plain site for thousands of years.

We see it in everyday life. What you put into the universe returns. The Karmic Scales of Justice. People build vision boards, meditate on them, recite mantras, try to set their intention to the universe, and then wait for directions or signs to achieve those visions. With the universe and the scales of justice, selfishness or greed does not create on God's side, so be very careful where you are setting your intentions.

Earth's Cardinal Alignments

It's important to understand the divine universal relationships, the pineal gland, and the energy power of earth to further understand why this is pertinent to the celestial alignment of the ancient landmarks. Any Google search or history book will tell you that the earth is approximately 4.5 billion years old and is constantly growing and evolving through its own gradual tectonic and volcanic activity and the effects of climate change. Neanderthal-like fossils have been found to be between 40,000 and 430,000 years old, which indicates that the beginnings of ancient civilizations are also within that time frame. Cardinal alignments have also changed in that time frame due to earth growth and shifting along its orbital axis. Even though the north pole has been documented with the most change in location, over time, spiritual sites in ancient civilizations follow the cardinal alignments, and each of these sites harbors a unique energy sensation.

A few of the most popular "high energy" places are Bali, Stonehenge, Egypt Pyramids, Machu Picchu, Himalayan mountains, Maui and other areas like the Grand Canyon, Sedona, Mount Shasta in California or Lake Louise in Alberta, Canada.

Landmarks that align on the grid generally have cardinal alignments, which are the north-south polarity and the east-west rising and setting of the sun. Equinoxes are a focus due to the significance of astronomy and the changing of seasons. Equinox and moon cycles do increase energy, although all sites with spiritual energy were utilized every day, not just on special occasions. Ancient civilization hieroglyphics display the most graphic account of vortex usage for portal travel or energy.

To understand the cardinal alignments with celestial grid lines and landmark placement, we need to think of the advanced species that brought us here from other universes where a solar system was dying. Although mankind has developed a fear of alien life and technology, we need to look back at the beginning of intelligent life on earth when that alien technology or "brain" power was linked to the control and use of energy to achieve great feats and to help ancient civilizations develop or be sustained. Brain power refers to an awakened pineal gland. We have seen many movies that depict these beginnings and the wars for power.

The movie "Knowing" is a science fiction film where the plot surrounds children who can tell when the world's natural disasters kill people and tell the end of our solar system. It also shows an alien connection to ships retrieving species to transport to other solar systems to save and preserve them, including two children, who are taken to a new world. The similarities to Adam and Eve's story.

Divine information is saying this depiction of ships transporting species is reality. Advanced ancient civilizations were started on earth by being brought here from other solar systems, by act of God(s) and advanced species that to us are extraterrestrial. When these civilizations were brought here, they would then know that a time would come for them to leave. Kind of like a rapture, except they willingly leave to start somewhere anew. Having been brought here, they also understood the "energy" required to get them here. They understood that earth had a natural resonance, a natural energy that, combined with their advanced brains, could be harnessed and used to build civilizations that paid tribute and worship to the universe, realms and dimensions. With this hypothesis, we need to accept that energetic travel is possible through wormholes, black holes, portals, vortices, celestial grid lines, and earth's natural forces with polar magnetism. Time travel, quantum travel, astral projection, lucid dreaming, whatever we want to call it, is possible.

Science has even looked at it with Nikola Tesla, Einstein, Stephen Hawkings, and current-day astrophysicists making claims about the possibilities.

Through my channeled insights, I am guided to investigate the discovered spiritual places on earth. As they are "discovered," they are now protected ancient landmarks that attract an abundance of tourism.

Almost every major ancient spiritual location is built on an energetic anomaly, with cardinal alignment references and celestial grid or leyline alignments. Other similarities include large precision stones, shaped and placed to perfection, higher frequency resonances, magical healing sensations or links to spiritual worship, proximity to tectonic plates and fault lines and underground water sources where geothermic energy is increased. People are drawn to these sites and have a feeling of magnetic pull, or attraction to the energetic frequency and feel "something" change within them there.

The random patterns of these vortices have spinning energy either in an upward or downward direction. Geospirals that have been studied so far have an upwelling, counterclockwise rotation, which we refer to as being positive energy or downward flowing. Clockwise rotation seems to be able to create negative feelings in a person who spends time near them, so we refer to them as negative energy. The more study placed in these sites, reveals overwhelming evidence that the ancients had a clear understanding of this energy grid system. Some indigenous cultures refer to these vortex locations as sacred and keep them protected. However, I will not go into detail about Indigenous sites.

The discovery of spiritual energy grids is generally verified with dowsing rods and confirmed with a "sensitive" who can communicate with the spirit realm. Energy vortices NEED to be taken seriously, as studies have found that overexposure in a positive vortex can cause overstimulation, inflammation, nervousness, and general restlessness and in a negative vortex, energy drain or weakening effect, lowering the immune system.

Divine information about the vortex I am aware of. It is a positive vortex. I have been given strict instructions for its activation and the amount of maximum time that can be spent in the "activation." Along with the maximum time frame, my instructions include being organic, no jewelry, no shoes, nothing electronic inside the "circle," and not going in with others, but do not visit the vortex alone. A "sensitive" in an activated vortex can open portals that are associated with it. A portal that can be dangerous in relation to the realms and dimensions or other portal locations that are still open or can still be activated. This includes access to those realms and for beings in those realms to access you. It also means getting lost and not finding your way back. There is a specific process to activation, which protects people who stumble into them unknowingly.

This is why many known vortex locations are protected or have prohibited or restricted access due to the higher presence of supernatural phenomena or high-energy anomalies.

The concepts of vortices and portals often fall within the realm of pseudoscience, spiritual beliefs, and fringe theories. These ideas are not supported by mainstream science and are frequently associated with various paranormal, mystical, or esoteric beliefs, for example:

1. Vortices: In some New Age and metaphysical beliefs, a vortex is considered a place where the Earth's energy is concentrated and flows in a spiral motion. These locations are often said to have heightened spiritual or healing energy.

Popular locations associated with vortices include Sedona in Arizona, USA. Mount Shasta in California, USA, and Lake Louise, Alberta, Canada.

2. Portals: Portals, in various cultural and mystical contexts, are thought to be gateways or entrances to other dimensions, realms, or realities. In paranormal and fringe theories, some suggest that specific locations or phenomena serve as portals to supernatural realms.

While certain sites may have cultural or spiritual significance, claims about vortices and portals as sources of specific energies or gateways to other realms have not yet been substantiated by scientific evidence. However, if we look at some of the myths and stories associated with the Grand Canyon for example, The Grand Canyon is a natural geological formation where there have been claims about supernatural phenomena in the area. A couple of examples of myths associated with the Grand Canyon are:

- Some individuals and groups suggest that the Grand Canyon is the site of mysterious energy vortices or portals to other dimensions. According to these claims, the alleged supernatural properties are said to be responsible for strange occurrences or heightened spiritual energy in certain areas of the canyon.

- There are myths suggesting that certain areas of the Grand Canyon are off-limits to the public due to supernatural or extraterrestrial activities. Some versions of this myth propose that the government is hiding evidence of paranormal phenomena.

The celestial grids and alignment of ancient civilization temples, tombs and other landmarks are interconnected to an energy grid that supports energetic travel between them through vortex portals, which also involves advanced use of the brain (pineal gland) for telekinesis, telepathy, and remote viewing.

Some of the most significant ancient civilization landmarks are aligned on a celestial grid. The four that I will focus on are Machu Picchu, Easter Island, Stonehenge and Egyptian pyramids. Each has a connection to vortices and portals. I will share a summary of the landmark and then the divine interpretation.

Machu Picchu

Historians state that Machu Picchu is a sacred and exclusive place where deities were worshipped. The cardinal alignments, and reference to the cathedral enclosure worshipping the four elements. The Incas religion was rooted in a polytheistic belief system. Gods were embodied in the elements of nature: the sun, moon, earth, and stars. Each element held a unique spiritual symbolism.

The Inca believed in three realms: the upper world, the earthly realm, and the underworld. These 3 realms also demonstrate the divine connection between 3 - 6 - 9. In relation to alignment – The north represents worship to God, The south to satanic ritual and the north Milky Way for teaching. Satanic rituals in this time period pertain to when Satan was still a god, the God of Death, which at that time symbolized the afterlife – good and bad. Satan, at the beginning, did not represent Evil. It's ironic, though, that a meme would describe something going wrong or bad as "Going south."

Tourists who go to Machu Picchu also claim there are certain spots or points where there is greater energy. Energies are enhanced by the vortex it was built on and the placement of the stones and windows to draw in the polar energies and absorb or rebound them to a concentrated meditation or worship area.

Temple of the Sun

The Temple of the Sun, also known as the Torreón, is one of the structures at Machu Picchu that align with the cardinal points. This temple is situated at the northern end of the site, has a north-south orientation, and is thought to have served as an astronomical observatory. The Temple of the Sun is specifically aligned with the solstices, and its windows and niches are positioned to capture the sunlight during significant solar events.

The circular wall is perfectly sectioned. Between the walls, you can see the windows. The windows acquire greater importance thanks to the tall stone that is found inside the temple. The strategic placement of the temple allows the sun's rays to enter during the solstices. The placement also allows for the concentration and trapping of polar and vortex energy.

The sculpture projecting from the rock bottom of the Sun temple is interpreted as "Water Mirrors for Observing the Sky."

 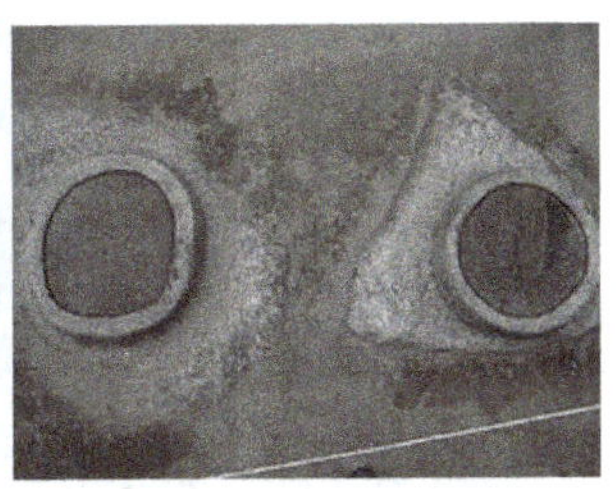

Divine Interpretation: The Temple of the Sun was used as a gathering place for teaching when travelers came back. They would teach about the other civilizations encountered and if they advanced in time, would teach about what they saw in the future. Visiting the ruins in Egypt was common. Int. Mach 'ay was the place where leaders would gather to learn about their travels and future.

Temple of 3 Windows and Principal Temple

The Room of the Three Windows and the Principal Temple is located in the sacred plaza and features three trapezoidal windows that align with the cardinal points. The windows are positioned to face east, providing views of the sunrise, and are made with finely carved stone blocks.

The Principal Temple, with its north-south alignment and central location, is made up of three stone walls in a 'U' shape, a structure called 'huayrana.' In the central part, there is a platform where, according to the researchers, the most important religious ceremonies were held in the citadel. In the upper part, there is a set of niches, seven in the central part and five in the side walls, where gold and silver objects are placed. For this reason, this construction is also known as the 'Templo Mayor.' All these structures had their central axis in the Main Temple, where the most important ceremonies and social events of the citadel were held. The base of the temple is made up of large lithic stones, which support more regular-sized and precisely carved stones.

In hieroglyphics, scenes of Pharoah or Queens are seen holding rods or a bag which contains the elements (metals) needed as conductors or absorbers of energy. They are also seen holding the bars of shungite and soapstone in their hands. Currently, the bags are thought to resemble a "man purse."

Temple of the Moon

The temple boasts niches and fake doors inserted in the stones beneath the overhanging cave, with an enormous 8-meter-high by 6-meter-wide entrance and a rock sculpted in the shape of an altar.

The temple is said to contain each of the three planes of the Inca religion: the Hanan Pacha (the heavens), the Kay Pacha (the earth), and the Ukju Pacha (the underworld), represented respectively by the condor, the puma, and the snake.

It has been speculated that the site was used for burials, a ceremonial bathing complex, or as an observation post due to the elevated position beneath the peak of Huayna Picchu on its north-western face.

Historical sources do note that the Inca perceived cave entrances as a place from which the first ancestors came and often buried their dead in caves so that the souls could return to reside there. The Inca also considered caves as sacred places for leaving offerings in dedication to the mountain deities.

Recent studies below the site support the theory of mountain worship, as archaeologists found a structure with two small holes cut into niches. When looking through the holes, the Cerro Yanantin is visible, which was also deified at sites such as Machu Picchu, where the Inca conducted rituals, and Pachamama's (offerings to the earth) at a shrine called the sacred rock that overlooked the Cerro Yanantin.

Divine Interpretation: The Temple of the Moon was used to tempt faith or where justice was served. Animal and people sacrifices were done here.

Temple of Condors

The Temple of the Condor is situated in the south eastern part of Machu Picchu and has a unique design. It's natural formation that is part of the mountain and managed to condition this "living rock" to resemble the open wings of a giant Andean Condor. The head and neck of the condor are carved on a stone altar at the feet of the Temple of the Condor.

when Cronos was still considered as the God of Death, which symbolized the afterlife – good and bad.

Intihuatana Stone

The Intihuatana stone, located near the Temple of the Sun (Torreón), is often considered a possible candidate for celestial alignments, including those with the Milky Way. The Intihuatana stone is a carved pillar that may have been used for astronomical observations, and its north - south orientation aligns with the cardinal points. Some researchers have proposed that the stone could have been used to observe the sun's zenith passage, and its orientation might have had connections to celestial events like the Milky Way's appearance in the night sky. Shamanic legends tell that when a sensitive person touches their forehead to the Intihuatana stone it opens their vision to the spirit world.

Divine Interpretation: The Intihuatana stone was used as a time stamp used to signify the amount of time, they could establish a connection with the gods. The gateway was only open at certain times of the day for a small window of time. It also tracked the time when portal energy could be activated and how long it would stay activated to allow passage in and out.

The divine explanation of the significance at Machu Pichu. There are 4 main temples at Machu Pichu, three of which represent the 3 Realms of worship. The north represents worship to God, The south to God of Death and the universe (Milky Way).

Stonehenge

Stonehenge is a prehistoric monument on Salisbury Plain in Wiltshire, England. It consists of an outer ring of vertical sarsen standing stones, each around 13 feet (4.0 m) high, seven feet (2.1 m) wide, and weighing around 25 tons, topped by connecting horizontal lintel stones. Inside is a ring of smaller bluestones. Inside these are free-standing trilithons, two bulkier vertical sarsens joined by one lintel. The whole monument, now ruinous, is aligned towards the sunrise on the summer solstice and sunset on the winter solstice. The stones are set within earthworks in the middle of the densest complex of Neolithic and Bronze Age monuments in England, including several hundred tumuli (burial mounds).

It has been suggested that Stonehenge may have been disassembled and rebuilt over the course of its existence, which coincides with the changing of the north pole locations due to the earth's rotational wobble. This change in pole alignment is best described by the articles published by Antiquity Reborn; Mario Buildrep's research on cardinal alignments and the ancient landmarks has the most accurate portrayal of Stonehenge's alignment in relation to its polar orientation at the time when it was built. The illustration below is from Antiquity Reborn's articles.

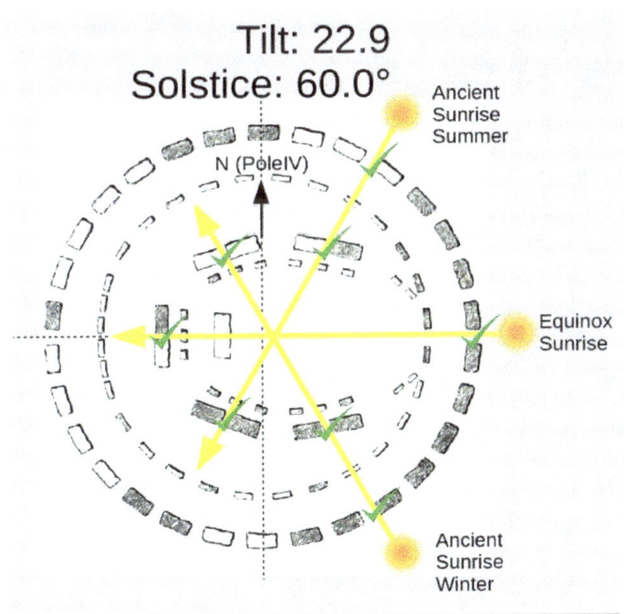

https://www.mariobuildreps.com/purpose-stonehenge/

Stonehenge portrays an energetic anomaly felt by almost all who visit there. (Unfortunately, combined with the groups of people who can access the site during solstice periods, the true energy amplification at site is not felt by the average person).

***Divine Interpretation**: Stonehenge is built upon a naturally occurring energy vortex, where the energy was used for meditation, healing, rituals, and portal travel. At the proper polar alignment, the magnetic field would pass and rebound off of the placement of the stones to the center of the circle, where the vortex anergy would be concentrated. The center was also used as an energy source to receive and transfer energy the same way ancient Egyptian civilization utilized the energy vortices within their palaces and pyramids to absorb and transfer energy and to portal or time travel. Once energy was absorbed, it could be used with the natural energy in the earth and atmosphere to achieve strength and mind power to move objects, heal or communicate with the other universal dimensions, thus the relationship to spiritual worship. The Equinox alignments also served as timekeepers and power boosters for energy. Today at Stonehenge, with the change in alignments, researchers find a notable sound resonance rebounding from the rock formations, leading scientists to believe Stonehenge was a place of healing based on sound waves. The current alignment does not produce the same results in energy creation. Stonehenge would also have holes for elements used to activate and amplify the vortex energy.*

Easter Island

Easter Island is another location of mystery with its nearly 1,000 extant monumental statues, called moai.

Divine Interpretation: The civilizations of this island (like Machu Picchu) were brought here from another solar system, and also knew that their time here was temporary until their extraction to their permanent location. There are no temples here, as we see in other landmark locations, but the statues represented the Gods from their culture. The gods look towards the sea, as protection from outsiders and to the inland as protection to the sea dwellings. The first inhabitants here were not like the average or normal humanoids that we currently relate to. This species was on a secluded island, close to the ocean for a reason. They primarily lived in the water but could exist on land as well. Most artifacts and dwellings will be in the ocean, not on land. The vortex energy would have been in the center of the most concentrated statue presence found with the seven Moai at Ahu Akvi that face outward towards the sea and face the point at which the sun sets during an equinox. Cardinal Alignments play significance when the vortex is the most energized, and the portals are activated.

Similar to Ancient Egypt, writing on stone has been found and is referred to as Rongorongo (pron. /ˈrɒŋɡoʊˈrɒŋɡoʊ/; Rapa Nui: Roŋoroŋo [roŋoˈroŋo]).

Angel Nuphriel KGW deciphers hieroglyphics for me, so we pulled illustrations from a Google search, "easter island hieroglyphics."

Knowing that the civilization was sea creature-based, the drawings start to make sense. Keep in mind that vortex portals bring "People" and the people are drawn as they appear to this civilization. As you will see in the Egyptian chapter, their people are often wearing headwear that looks like antlers.

These are the deciphers according to Angel Nuphriel KGW and deciphered from left to right and from top row to bottom row. (Traditionally, they would be done bottom to top in a linear presentation).

Top Row

Saw at the portal, people to get people to go with them. People only want females to go. They want to show them how females in other civilizations live. People are only female; people are from other civilizations. People are friendly, waving. Only want females to go.

2nd row

Slowly approach. Slowly go ahead. Only people who are important. People are men carrying three canteens. They stay, and men teach about other people in other civilizations. Taking people to show what their men do in their land. People friendly. People are a pleasure to see.

3rd row

Saw people. Quite a different civilization. People more men after people of importance. Females take females to the portal. People upside-down, upside-down female and one male. Friendly female, friendly male (coming through portal upside down is a way to show friendliness – shows silliness).

4th row

People sitting at portal. People taking people to portal. People want to make love with other people from other civilizations. People only want males. People hugging, stay one day. People stretching, more people male and female. People stay and make love.

Last Row

At portal, people upside down. Stop. Only people with big shoes of importance. People upside down. People take people at portal, people upside down. People friendly. People only men. People males only want people (sea creatures) making fun of them.

This illustration was taken from Wikipedia, and I asked Angel Nuphrial KGW what the meanings were.

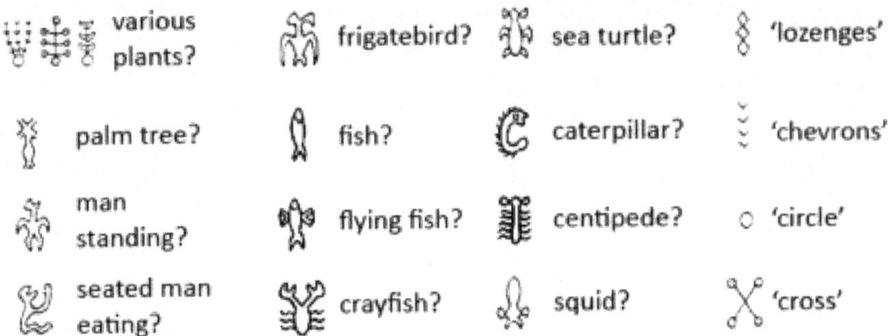

Angel Nuphriel KGW deciphers these as follows:

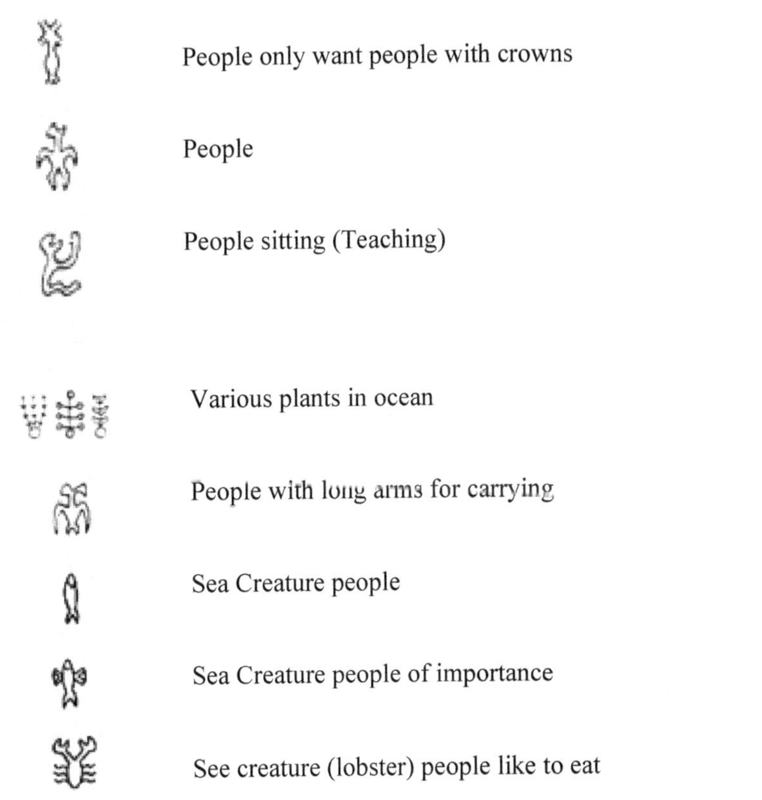

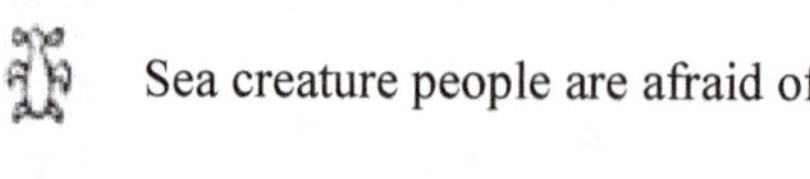   Sea creature people are afraid of

      Sea creature people are afraid of

      Sea creature (shrimp) people like to eat

      People with big heads (Egyptians seen with big heads or aliens)

      Of importance

      Portal

      Stop

      Criss Cross – Portal entry - Exit

Other distinct features of the sea creature people. Females are shown with long fins, whereas males are shown with genitals. Communication was through telepathic thought using pictures.

Female

Male

Ancient Egypt

Pyramids were also built in orientation to the cardinal points, with emphasis to the north.

The significance of alignment and 3 - 6 - 9 represents the worship of God, Universe and Satan. Pyramid shape is an equilateral triangle, and the entrances and corridor alignment of the pyramids to the north allowed the energy power to enter and resonate to be absorbed or reflected to be used or stored, and the equinox relationship to portal openings and other ceremonial factors. The entrance direction to the burial tombs depicted who they worshiped and the "Face" side of the pyramid. The portals existed in the tombs at the pyramids and at palaces. They paid high honor to the afterlife, and the portals allowed family members and consorts to communicate and receive guidance with their leaders and ancestors from the afterlife. The portals also supported the arrival and departures of other civilizations.

The key similarities to ancient civilizations across the globe is an example of the portal travel and education from one civilization to another.

The portal locations for many of these civilizations were closed at their departure and remain closed. At the rise of the Roman Empire, Romans wanted the power only to be for themselves. As they conquered, only the people who served the higher rulers of the empires, were allowed to use their pineal gland for higher power as prophets.

Message from Eric M

There is so much detail of earth power in Ancient Egyptian hieroglyphics that I dedicated an entire chapter to a sample of how they utilized and recorded earth energy.

Time or linear portal travel is not so far-fetched when glyphs from various ancient civilizations make reference to portals and visitors, and there is current research into time travel. Time travel is one of the most sought-after explanations in the scientific world. Recorded concepts of research on this subject began with Einstein and Nikola Tesla and continued with renowned research by Steven Hawkins and several philanthropy studies at worldwide universities. You can find articles via google and look into all the fiction, science fiction novels, movies or TV shows on the concept of time travel. Tik Tok has even brought out stories or warnings from time travelers.

As a side story, Ancient Egyptian hieroglyphics refer to time travelers Jedi and are usually shown with caution or by a fire. They were distractions as teaching and learning occurred with the arrival of a Jedi.

We have also seen questionable resemblances about the future in some hieroglyphics showing helicopters, submarines, tanks etc.

Watching "The Sacred Geometry" series on Gaia, I find it ironic that there is a connection between the Jedi symbol used in hieroglyphics to the Jedi lightsaber handle, which was introduced in the Star Wars movies. It is also interesting that Google returns results stating that a Jedi is a person who shows extraordinary skill or expertise in a specified field or endeavor. They are revered as guardians of peace and justice in the galaxy. As mystical wielders of the "Force" (the Force, known as the "Power of Cosmos" and was a metaphysical, spiritual, binding, and ubiquitous power).

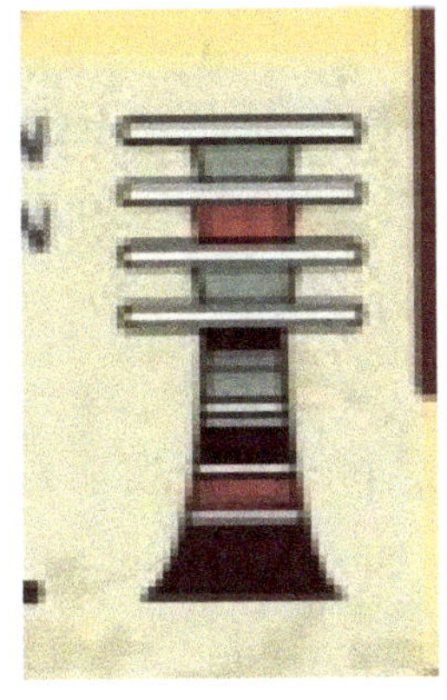 

The significance of this relationship to Jedi being a time traveler in Ancient Egypt related to the four aspects defined by prominent Jedi philosophies: The Living Force dealt with the energy of living things; the Unifying Force, with the entirety of time and space; the Cosmic Force, with life after death; and the Physical Force, with anything within one's surroundings. Others thought of the Force as an entity capable of intelligent thought, almost as a sort of deity. Though the Force was thought to flow through every living thing, its power could only be harnessed by beings described as "Force-sensitive." Force-sensitive beings were able to tap into the Force to perform acts of great skill and agility as well as control and shape the world around them. Sometimes, this ability was described as having a strong Force "aura."

I make reference to Star Wars, as it's another movie comparison, and enthusiasts will understand the "Force" relationship.

Divine communications indicate that time travel was possible and still is and utilized the earth energy power and vortex locations to travel. The portals activated in a Vortex had narrow windows of time, very specific to be in the portal and return, which is why we see a prominence of timekeeping with sundials etc.

Nikola Tesla was also obsessed with the Egyptian pyramids, and believed they were giant transmitters of energy. He built his Towers known as "Tesla's electromagnetic pyramid" based on their design. He believed there was a relationship between earth's energy, the elliptical orbit of the planet and the equator. The pyramids are a power transmitting device, except for vortices and portals within the pyramids or other power receiving/transmitting sites (palaces) served as the centers to "amp up" with power or to receive or transmit the required energetic strength.

Ancient civilizations calculated power needs by observation of the natural environments around them. Hieroglyphics show that in symbolism, for example, animal, weather, earth elements or manpower.

Manpower is calculated in strength by royalty (Pharaoh, Queen, Princess, Prince, or children in waiting), slaves (which they referred to as monkeys), in addition to animal strength or mannerisms.

Power is measured by how much manpower is needed to lift, move, and set down an object. Also figures in energy deflections (interferences), or other elements like water, hot sand, or when the energy transmission needs to be cooled down or heat protected.

Note: The hieroglyphic symbol for a slave is a monkey, which refers to something easy or simple to do. Even in our current memes we say, "a monkey could do it." The Monkey symbol is used a lot in hieroglyphics, so here are some examples of monkeys in hieroglyphics. The way they are facing also determines direction:

This is an illustration from the Scientific Research Journal, Archaeological Discovery Vol.11 No.1 January 2023, "The Role of Abolishing Gravity in Ancient Egyptian Pyramids Architecture."

https://www.scirp.org/journal/paperinformation.aspx?paperid=122713

This illustrates the calculation for manpower to lift, carry and set down the Pharoh Statue. Manpower is then converted into how much earth energy/frequency is needed to be absorbed to control the gravitational resistance and velocity of motion. The information for deciphering this diagram came from the channeling of Angel Nuphriel KGW.

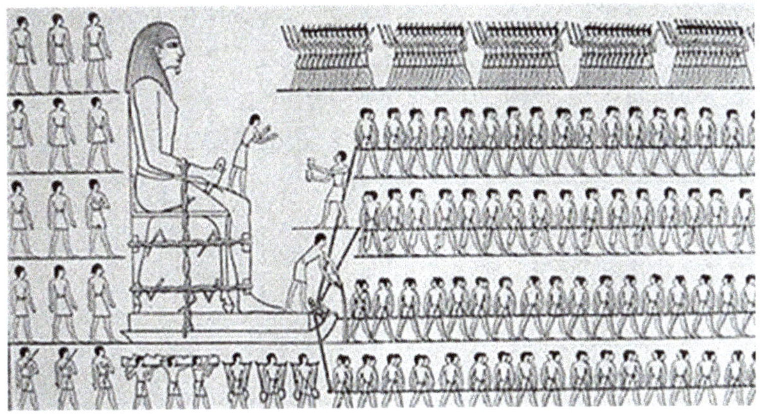

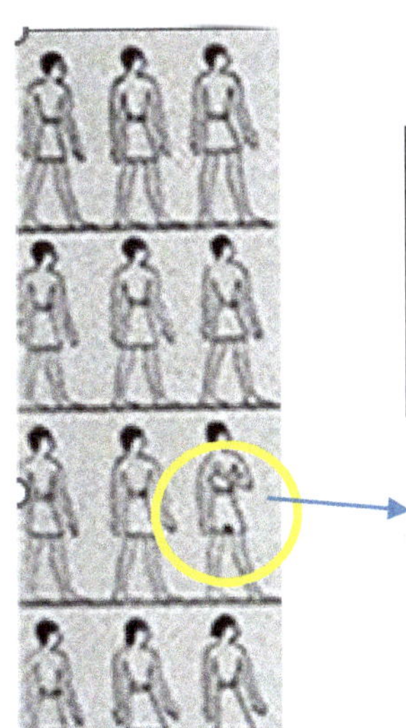

These men represent royalty, which can absorb and transfer more energy to one another or to the object
There are 4 rows of men, with three in each row
The power represented is the power of 4 men amplified 3 times

One Power direction to north, north – south alignments are significant for energy power

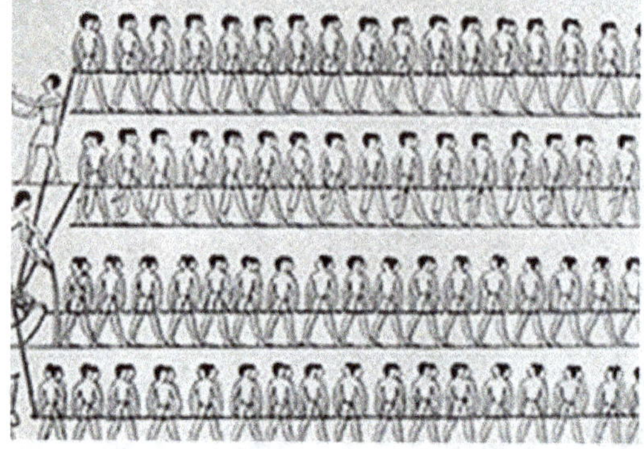

These men (monkeys) are how much
power of their strength is needed
to move statue

If the diagram was complete there
would be
power of 4 amplified by 100 men

One power to give directions
One power directing power
One power to control ropes

If drawing was complete
there would be 6 boats

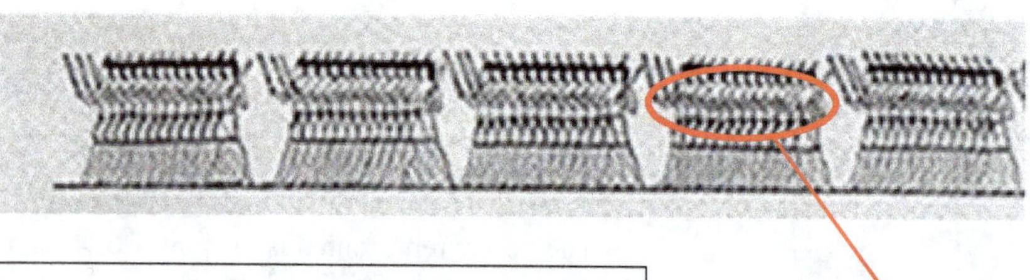

2 rows of men, 14 in each row
Power of 2 men amplified by 28 to carry 6
boats

Twelve persons rowboat

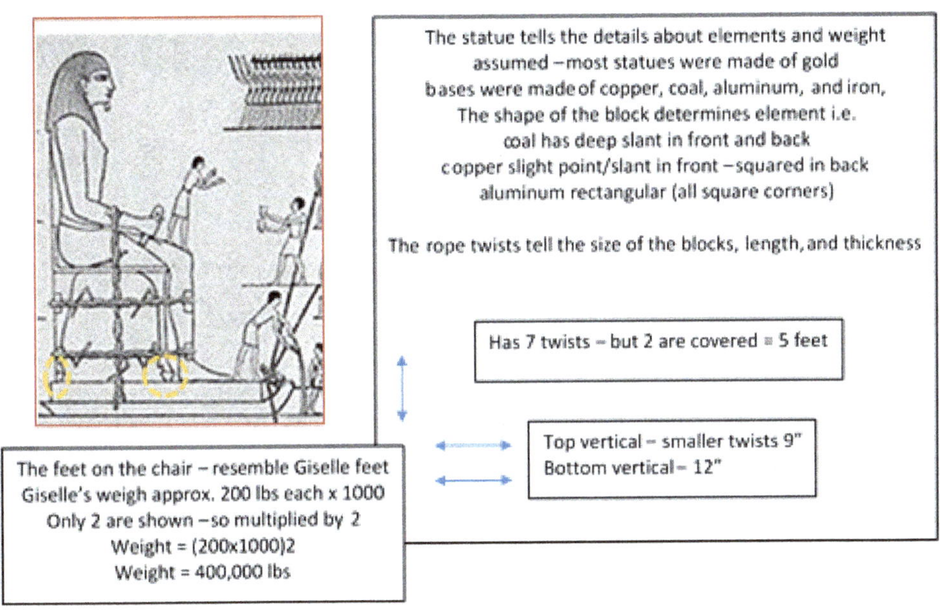

The calculated amount of people to move this structure is 18.

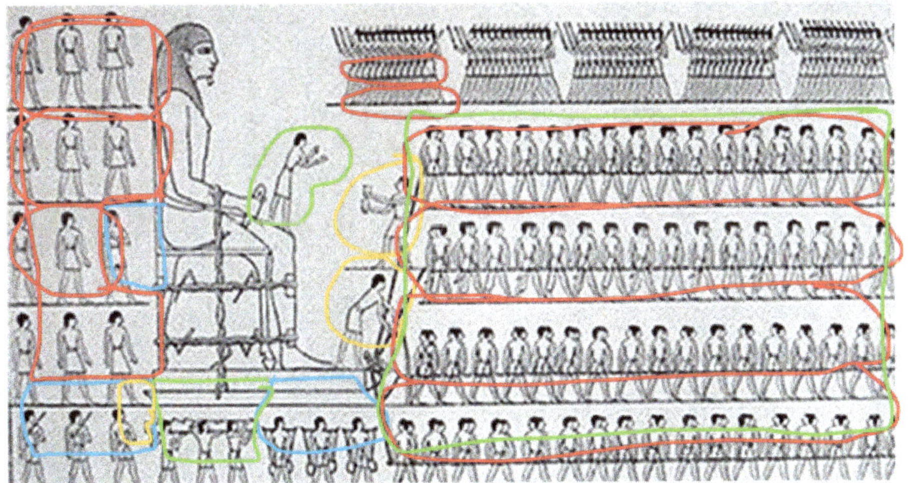

Power Symbols

As to not discredit previous attempts to decipher hieroglyphics
into an alphabet or phonic language, I remind you that I am being

mentored by a spirit angel named Nuphriel KGW (Angel of Mentors), and these are his channelings.

The symbols of power are not necessarily the Pharoh's authoritative power. It's the amount of earth power/frequency required or how to use the earth power in which direction.

The Crook and Flail is currently interpreted as a Pharoh's symbolism or power of authority to rule and control his herd (royal family and slaves).

The Flail, shown with multiple rods, represents the distance his power is capable of reaching. The Crook, depending on the direction of the open end – moves the levitated object in that direction. The third is a scoop which is used to lift and lower an object. The actual power represented by the Crook, Flail, and scoop is unimaginable.

Places of importance, like palaces and pyramids, were built on vortex energy fields, so energy could be directed from any vortex location.

Even a sarcophagus describes the power the pharaoh (or occupant) was capable of.

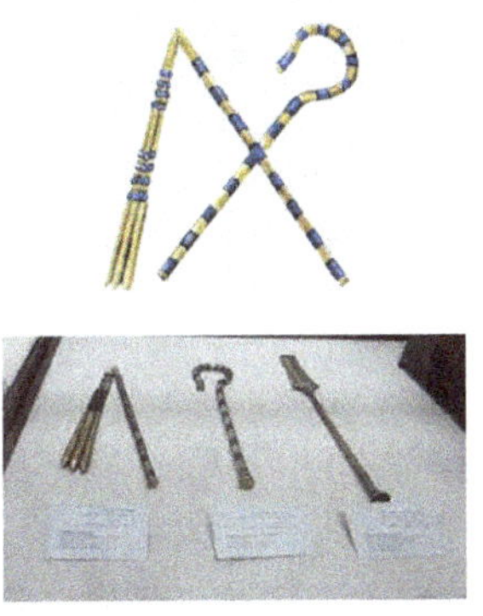

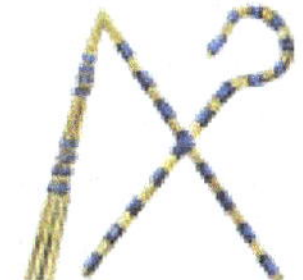

The Divine Interpretation included the amp or amplifier power for each element, with respect to earth energy, but has been deliberately left out in these "Power" Illustrations. These amps,

Power symbols are represented in various ways in the
hieroglyphics. How much power, what direction of power, when
to dump power and when to reload. The elements, earth amps,
earth watts, earth voltage and the amplifiers and grounding used
are also shown.

This illustration is an example of a princess receiving power from
a queen. Almost every detail in their clothing, headdresses, and
manner represents the type of power and measure of power.

*The diagram shown below tells two different stories at the same
time. The hieroglyphic in the background, and the colored detail
one. The center images of the queen and princess depict the
energy power. The hieroglyphic story contains power symbols,
which are seen in almost all hieroglyphics. They've been circled
in the illustration below, and depending on the direction they are
facing, the alignment with either north or south. Each line, dot,
hexagon, wavy or straight line, circle or tube, and color indicates
a detail to the power in earth energy/frequency terms. The width
of the shape and the count of feathers, hexagons, dots, blocks etc.
give details of the strength.*

Note: The feather, as it is sometimes difficult to see the lines, represents
$1P^8$ (1 man with a power of 8). The stock of wheat, 4 leaves and shaft
represent $1P^5$ (1 man with a power of 5).

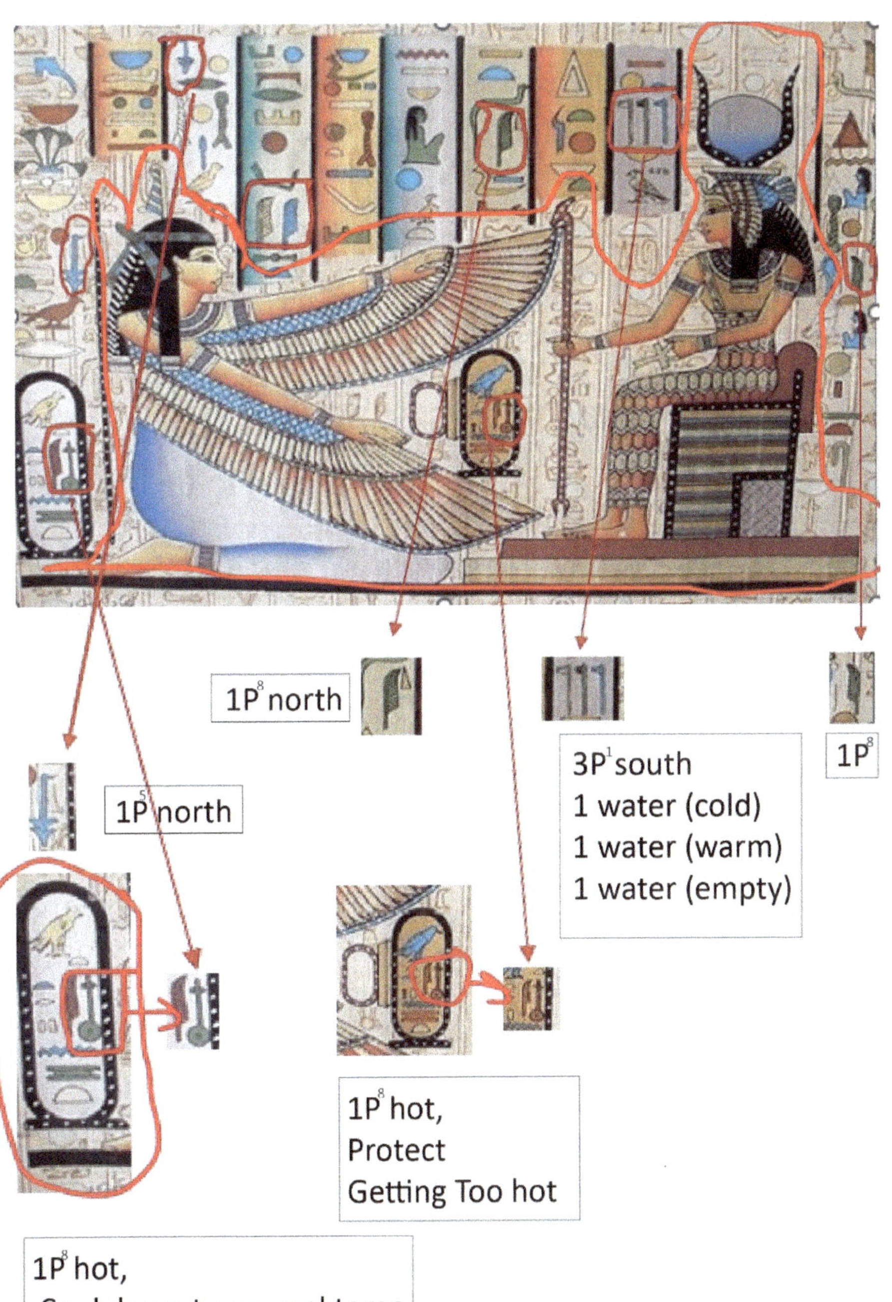

1P⁸ north
1P⁵ north
3P¹ south
1 water (cold)
1 water (warm)
1 water (empty)
1P⁸
1P⁸ hot,
Protect
Getting Too hot
1P⁸ hot,
Cool down to normal temp

This illustration is about a queen, who is absorbing earth power/frequency into her body and cells within and transferring power to the princess for her assignment, which obviously involves flight.

When the picture color has been enhanced, it is easier to recognize the elements (Aluminum, copper, bronze, zinc, iron, coal, earth) and the power (volts, amps, amplifier, grounding, absorbing) etc. Remember, we are not talking about mechanical power or electrical power as we know it today.

Orange   (Amplifier)

Blue (Amps)

Yellowish (Power of)

Colors in the illustration

Clay (dirt = grounding)

Goldish (Aluminum (used as amplifier))

Peach (Copper (amps))

Black (Coal (used to absorb energy))

Blue (Bronze (Amps))

Grey (Zinc (absorbs)

Elements and metals shown in the drawings represent what they are, for example, Amps, Volts, amplification, absorption, and grounding. Angel Nuphriel KGW provided the amount of amps and amplification, however, for safety reasons, we don't want people running around with copper or aluminum rods and sticking them in the ground anywhere when they don't know what they are for.

Copper, Uranium, Bronze and Brass create amps. Aluminum amplifies the energy. Coal and Zinc absorb energy, and earth/clay and cork are grounding.

On top of her head are two antlers (Antenna) made of coal
There are 22 dots in total (Balance with 11 each side). Each dot represents volts

The globe is a conductor, made with sand, limestone and water
The size of globes or orbs determine the amp power.

The globe and antenna are balanced on a plate (Amplifier) with a base of Bronze and Zinc (Absorbs) 5 Zinc 6 bronze

The crown head piece represents the type of power she is giving
Goose – fly in formation, sometimes circling, but steady
Each part of the goose (head, wind, butt, and tail feather) has it's own type of power
Goose head – amplifier
Wing is separated 4 times with bronze and the wing color indicates It's an amplifier (Aluminum)
Outer wing (larger) with Bronze separator
Column to left – smaller –amplifier bronze separator
Next column amplifier bronze separator
Neck amplifier
Blue Butt – Bronze 11 feathers
Blue tail feathers Bronze – 2 separate
2 together double power

Queens hair has tubes down the back that are
Solid aluminum 3" by ½" act as receivers

Necklace has 5 rings, each ring represents power
Outer Aluminum narrow ring
Bronze Zinc nodules
Aluminum ring
Bronze zinc longer nodule
Aluminum ring

Queens Dress is iron, copper and aluminum
Each brownish hexagon shape is copper
Each goldish hexagon Aluminum
The shoulder strap, top strip and bottom strips are iron
Some of the hexagons are ½, ¾ or ¼ size
The wavy line separator accounts for deviation as
when aluminum and copper conduct there is a deviation
Iron charge plate

Starting from bottom of dress
Row of iron
3 half hexagon and ¼ = 1¾ amplified
3 ½ way line deviation
3 ¾ copper
4 wavy line deviation (count peak as 1)
4 Aluminum
4 coppers
4 wavy lines
4 Aluminum
And so, on up the dress. When there is an arm
Covering – those don't count

Her Scepter is made of copper, and 3 components
And each dot represents volts.
Head at top (pointing down at, and touching
The princess) – 3 dots
Shaft – 33 dots
The 2 prongs at bottom – 2 dots

Her 2 feet represent distance between the
Queen and Princess for the power transfer

Other jewelry – is just jewelry
Hair in front of necklace is not an interruption
The Looking Key – pointing direction of power release

The color of her skin is a warm/hot transfer

The Chair and Base is a power source on its own – that the queen is absorbing power from, each color Represents an element with its own charge

Width and length of each block or line equal strength of power (Bottom is ½ of top)
And the base Earth, Aluminum, Copper, and Coal

The glyph to the left is an interruption that occurred due to the energy transfer.

Meant to be read from the bottom to top

Straight away
Empty Sand
Empty Water
2 days – Power of 1 Heated – Power down to cool
Deflected
Levitation
Sand
In an instant

The Princess Receiving the Power tells her own story of earth power/frequency.

Aluminum tubes in hair are receivers

Necklace with 5 Aluminum rings
1 ring of 10 nodules
and 1 ring 20 nodules

Wings (receiving power of lift)
Each dot in the blue area is amps
– Blue means cold
Lines in between amplifiers (by 10)
The feathers are the power of men
Goldish (Warm)– each feather $10P^{100}$
Orange/Yellow (Hot)each feather $1P^{100}$

Her foot is pointing to south, and
her dress is she staying cold

There is an interruption to the power transfer indicated
By the symbolism touching her wing and situated between them

12 dots (volts) connected to princess
(Touching wing)
Ground 14 dots (Volts)
Copper conduit s allows transfer to
Keep going

Copper/Aluminum plate to balance transfer

Events in an oval means Something occurred suddenly
This reads as follows from bottom up: (background color
means things getting very warm

In an instant
protection from sand
Heats up ground X2 creating deflection
one day – block – hot power to north – amp hot
Water hole in way
Block cold going straight

The Hieroglyphic story of what is "seen" in this illustration.

Most Hieroglyphic storyboards are written linear or vertically. When there is a central focal point, as in the above example, the instructions start at the bottom left and work their way around the scene. There are separator lines, sometimes boxes or in an oval, which indicates that there is something specific or suddenly came up that directions need to be altered. In the illustration above, there are two different stories being told, as you can see a different set of hieroglyphics in the background. Storyboards represent a vision board, a way to set intent and energy to objects and people involved in the movement of goods and services.

Read from bottom to top:

At water pond, stay walking straight and protect from the warm water and watch, king's army approaches from south. Hot sun more power of cold power to north is needed. Sand pit, meet at the poisonous plants and hot sand pit under the waterfall

Read from top to bottom:

It's very hot and warm: Cold water pit, need one arms length of time in day and one arm length of time at night for warm and cold water. Go around west and block heat to protect warm water in the storm. Stay hot and need power of water and sand to the south three times.

Read from bottom to top:

Go straight around to the north for 2 days, cold temperatures, Criss-cross empty around, sun at night and criss-cross warm, At warm water pond, Cold power of five south with sun at night.

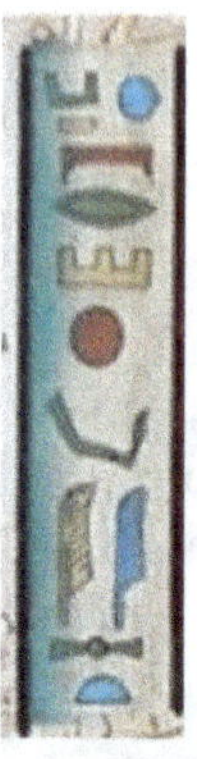

Read from top to bottom:

It will be wet and cold: Block warm empty pit from cold water. stay under tent at warm water hole. King approaches. Warm up in the hot sun by crook in road. Get power of 8 of sand and power of 8 cold water, meet and protect from cold rainstorm.

Read from bottom to top:

It's very hot and warm. King army approaches, at bend in road, stay cold. Protect from warm sun, crisscross hot, stay one day. hot sun blocks of sand and water, searther (split energy) at cold water hole

Read from top to bottom:

It is wet and cool: hot deflection, stay at sand pit, monkey (slave) waiting for north directions cold, water hole waddle like a duck to protect from light storms

Read from bottom to top:

It's warm: one arms length of time at night. Searther (split energy) to block cold. Slither around power of 8 warm by fire, Protect form cold weather, stay one night.

Read from top to bottom:

Very hot: double caution. protect from storm hot sun sears, protect sand from storm.

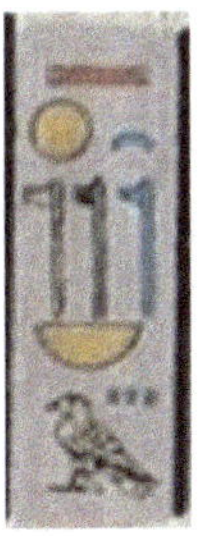

Read from bottom to top:

Cooler: straight for 3 days, at sand pit, power of 1 water empty south, power of 1 man warm south and power of 1-man cold south, sun at night, protect water, stay hot.

Read from top to bottom:

Power of eight warm south, slither around caution double hot sand deflection. Cold monkey waiting for directions south. Warm crisscross around sand pit crisscross. Cold temperature, power of 8 warm south protect from sandstorm. Monkey cold waiting for directions south. At sand hole, block hot, stay warm protect from heat storm.
go around north.

Sometimes during the deciphering, a meaning does not make sense. For example, *Waddle like a duck*. Why would anyone want to do that? Then, one day, my daughter and I were carrying a large shelf, and I had to drop my end, I was laughing so hard. The way we were shuffling our feet, from the awkwardness and weight, was exactly how I would picture a duck waddling and sidestepping (crisscrossing).

Other meanings In Hieroglyphics: when a bird is drawn, it refers to the mannerisms of the bird. For example, Owls fly in a searching pattern or are always looking around; hawks or falcons fly straight or in a direct path. A crane stands upright when spooked or takes long strides when it walks; a crow or raven likes to scavenge and steal things, so it's a caution when they are drawn; turkeys don't fly well and are clumsy or jumpy. A snake slithers around obstacles, a snail is slow, and a turtle is also slow and if on it's back is a standstill (can't move). Sometimes, a bullhead or entire bull is drawn, which can translate to a meme "Like a bull in a China shop". Or a pen is drawn with them to show they are out or to put them in. The more you approach the hieroglyphics with a child's eye view, the more they make sense. "Science" is trying too hard and complicating the translations.

When Angel Nuphriel KGW and I work on a diagram, it's always amazing to see the story unfold, but that will have to wait until the next book.

Behind the Scenes

The information contained in this writing will be controversial to some, and to some, a revelation that they may not be ready to hear or visualize. The concept of vortices, portals and divinity have long been locked away by religious groups, governments, and various cultures, and perhaps done so as a way to maintain power over or to protect the people. People believe that there is an alien presence on this planet, but the idea of extra-terrestrial influence is revered with fear or as a threat. Vortex portals are also viewed as threatening, not only as gateways for UFO and mystical creature activity, but a loss of control over the people entering an exiting portal location, and the threat or acts of violence that can be associated with it.

When I started the initial research into earth energy and earth frequency, it was with geothermal energy in mind. When those inquiries about earth energy and earth power led me to Nikola Tesla's research and the Schumann Resonance, and I began to dig deeper into it, my Divine team began to question my motives. They thought I was getting off track. But when the divinity connections also started to make sense, things took a different turn. Even the Divine team thought that Tesla's research, which in the end was targeted to make a weapon of destruction, was not a leap in the right direction, but with my reasoning, they too found the connections to 3 - 6 - 9 and the earth energy veil.

Earth energy and resonance are not a new concept. Using artificial electricity, laboratories have made technological breakthroughs in healing and disease treatment with scalar waves and sound frequency. The market is saturated with home machines. This EM scalar wave is a naturally occurring resonance within earth's frequency, energy and the celestial grid that can be tapped into just as ancient civilizations before us did. But it is to be regarded with respect and caution, as natural earth energy has risks associated with it if misused.

Much like the reference in the past to Moses or the story of Noah, God has stated that there is a purpose for this information to be written and shared. The Divine team guided me to focus on research and then filled in the gaps to make the connections.

At first, the writings were about hieroglyphics, but with every turn in research, they kept coming back to universal energy and divinity. The sample of Egyptian hieroglyphics in this book is only a sample of many illustrations that Angel Nuphriel KGW has deciphered with me, and I will eventually publish or teach more.

I made a daily routine of channeling my Divine team, and the more they shared, the more far-fetched some things seemed, but then again, the more everything made sense and presented a logical, believable explanation.

My intent is not to debunk history or make a claim that any other research is false or wrong. Science and history are based on what we see and the initial interpretations of such from that person's view. Even the bible is a compilation of observations written from the author's viewpoint. I'm only offering another alternative for "science" and historians to explore.

When I started this, I already believed in the Spirit realm and felt that there was a God or something in the universe that was Divine.

There are lost souls in the world. Those who believe there is a God or something that makes everything living thing possible but do not follow a structured, organized, ritualistic religion. It doesn't matter which representation of God you believe in as long as you believe. Although I don't follow an organized religion or go to church, I am encouraged to enter at least a church that I am comfortable with and pray.

I was an example of a lost soul. I was baptized into a religion I do not faithfully follow. I attended a church once in a while with a grandparent or friend when I was young. Otherwise, I only entered a church for a wedding, baptism, or funeral. I attempted catechism in primary school, which I did not complete, although I taught myself and learned the prayers of the Rosary, as the bible refers to those prayers and I thought they were important, and at times they gave me comfort. From a spiritual sense, I recognized the importance of grounding and surrounding myself with the white golden light of protection and other invocations when I meditate or practice healing with Reiki. I didn't think I was good at meditation because I generally fell asleep. I had lucid dreams where Satan tried to tempt me, but in those lucid dreams, I was aware and was always able to maintain my faith and love for God, profess my love and choice to choose God, and those prayers came in handy to make Satan back off. I have been attacked by Satan and his gurus in lucid dreaming and through prayer and professing my faith and love for God. I was able to let go and make them go away.

I am reminded of the story about the Wind and the Sun. They had a challenge to see who could get the coat off the man walking down the road. The wind blew as hard as he could and came at the man from all directions, whipping him around, but the man just held tighter to his jacket and persevered on. The sun shone gently and as bright as it could, surrounding the man with warmth. This made the man happy, but it also made him very hot, so he eventually took his coat off.

Let's reimagine this story with God and his son Lucifer. The greatest of family disputes. They don't agree on things and are at each other with competition and challenges. They see a lost soul, one that lives day to day questioning their purpose, questioning life in general, and just spiritually feeling lost. God and Lucifer have a challenge on who can influence that person more. They both offer great achievements that are possible, offer rewards, empty promises, add tests of loyalty and tests that offer things like fame and money that could lead to either greed or help mankind.

If you were this person, and you knew you were being tested, how do you choose? Is your unconditional love for God and humanity enough to stand up against Lucifer, or are you not strong enough because your fear and doubts are too strong and take over? Satan is looking for the weak, the insecure, doubtful, greed-stricken people. He wants to stack his "earth army" with them. Are you strong enough to face Satan and tell him you are not afraid of him, that you love God and follow God? Your strength to stand up to him is enough to weaken him. Prayer, meditation and singing give energy to the spirit realm. Love, unconditional love, gives God strength. Stand up to Satan, and tell him you do not fear him, that your love for God, his angels and spirits is far more powerful than he is.

I have visited Mystics before, read their books, and the books of others about heaven. The connections I've had with God, my Ancestral Guardian, Angel, Arch Angels, my dad, and other relatives, I know there is something there, and I will stand up and face Satan over and over to profess that I choose the right of choice, that involves judgement, redemption, and forgiveness and for my Soul to live on after my organic bodies die. In many encounters published about crossing over, there is always a recount of a life review, which also comes with feeling your own emotions and those of everyone else in every situation and learning the value of forgiveness the soul needs and how forgiveness releases so much in ourselves as well.

Another statement that I've encountered in other books from mystics or mediums is, "We (our soul) choose the lifepath to be born into, for our soul needs to find balance and understanding from actions and situations from our past experiences."

As much as I want to interfere with choices or detour from the soul's purpose, it's up to each individual born to figure out, learn and correct their route to their life plan. Most times, they do, although the road is very bumpy and painful, and sometimes they don't. It's powerful to recognize that when things are not going your way, you choose that upon yourself, and you have the power within you to correct or choose a different route.

A word about hate. A friend and I were talking about someone we disliked and used the word hate; their father overheard us talking and pulled us aside and said, "Hate takes up a lot of energy and emotion, more so than it takes to love someone. So why would you want to give up so much of your energy to someone you may not like in the current moment?" Those words stayed with me from that day forward. When situations came up where that hate emotion crept in, I consciously reminded myself that the person or situation did not deserve my energy, and instead, I prayed for them. Just something small like "God, please help them." And with the lesson about hate, I learned the value of unconditional love, which is not always easy.

There are human "angels" that walk amongst us. They are here to help save humanity and to maintain the value behind having a choice and having free will. They are here to bring us hope.

I've had the thought of "what if?" in the back of my mind that these channelings and this book are an indication of the potential for the "second coming" and wanting to preserve a different perspective of history? Or a warning to us that the next war between Heaven and Satan for rule will require humankind to be more "aware"?

There are innocent people unaware that they have contracted their souls to Satan. Social media has made it easy to lure people to buy into things, knowing people are looking for a quick fix to their problems or issues. The Divine team has indicated that a return to the pure soul at the moment of birth can cancel Satan's contract. Hypnotherapy and Natural earth energy scalar waves can accomplish that. Those who want to be certain to pass over into God's realm to face redemption, justice, forgiveness, and be reborn again will seek out the ones who can cancel contracts. Be reminded that a soul contract with Satan ends your soul's existence when your current organic body dies.

I have appreciation and great gratitude that I have been chosen to deliver these messages. I am also humbled that I can reach any spirit, angel, or God when I need guidance or simply someone to talk to. That is a special gift. As for Satan, I don't like when he interferes or intrudes with my channeling. He can do that because he once was a God and is still classified as an angel. I let him know he is not welcome, and I pray for him (which weakens him and makes him very angry). I also know he is watching me, curious as to why I have been chosen.

My Ancestral Guardian, Maximillian, asked that I close with this prayer.

"Please accept that the accounts of history I have written do not change your view of history as you have been taught. God wants you to know what transpired over the course of evolution and question people on their beliefs. People can make their own decisions on truth or fiction about God's word. People are indecisive about whether there is a God. People have free choice to accept the word of God, and they have the choice to decide for themselves. People don't want to be told to believe or not to believe. People need to know they have free choice, as that was the ultimate sacrifice made by Jesus."

***

Divine Team Conversations

There were many conversations with the spirit realm that didn't quite fit into a chapter within the book, but they are related to the research and lessons about earth energy and frequencies, and I thought a couple deserved some mention. Below are a few of my channeled conversations with my Divine team. Spirit words are in italics blue, and my responses are in black regular type.

Quantum Physics lesson from Erik M.

God wants me to help you understand quantum physics.

Like a tutor?

Something like that.

Ok.

Quantum physics is like getting spun around in a tunnel. The worst part of the momentum is what tells us the energy. Momentum is the result of the energy used, so energy is created by momentum from friction in the tunnel.

Ok, friction in a tunnel is like a piston in a chamber on a motor. The piston goes up and down, creating friction, which creates energy, which, in essence, runs the motor?

Yes, motors need friction to make energy. Momentum is achieved through energy which momentum is transferred to the wheel.

So, a piston in a chamber creates friction, which creates energy, which makes the engine run. Engine running, in turn, creates momentum or friction through a pulley (gear) system, which turns the drive shaft, which turns the wheels.

Yes, in quantum physics, the momentum is created by frequencies, which means momentum is achieved when a sound wave reaches a certain frequency it will cause something to move.

Is that like the slim or powder mass on a speaker? The sound makes the speaker move, which makes the slim move? (Wind chimes were chiming outside on the deck).

No, it's like a wind chime that makes a sound when the wind blows it. The sound travels in all directions, making it heard, but if the wind was not there, wind chimes would be still. So, a sound wave is like wind, except with no wind, and the sound makes things move, so a sound wave can have the same effect as wind.

OK, but something has to create the sound?

Earth creates its own sound wave.

Which is the 7.83 Hz or whatever, right?

OK, well, I knew there must have been a reason to buy those tuning forks.

Yes, we put that in your head.

How do I use the tuning forks to locate sound waves, and how do I know what frequency tuning fork to use?

You use the 4096, and when you tang it, it will react with the frequency of earth and create a sound wave that will create momentum that could make a wind chime move.

So, what you are saying is when my 4096 arrives, and I locate the vortex and I take a wind chime with me, I could create a sound wave to make the wind chime move?

Yes, that is what you need to do.

Can I just go to my front yard and do that? Would it create a sound wave to make the wind chime go?

Maybe, but you need to locate the vortex and try it there.

Could I record sound frequencies on my phone and then play them back in the vortex?

No, your phone will create feedback that construes the results.

Will any of the tuning forks I have work?

Yes.

Ok, which one?

512.

Ok, the 512. What will it do?

It will create a lower amount of electricity.

So, the higher the tuning fork, the better?

Yes, do you see now why we want you to study?

The conversation kept going to include more instructions for what to do in the vortex, but that's another story.

Message from God

You need to study more on earth energy and frequencies. Study momentum from sound waves, momentum from sound waves charges cells, fixing them where broken.

Broken cells equal disease etc. Can you explain the scalar chambers being used at healing centers? How does that differ from what I am researching?

Those centers use artificial electricity to create sound waves, but that creates too much interference with the organic body.

What about people who have metal plates or screws in their bodies from injury?

Metal plates will not affect scalar waves, but someone with a belly ring would distort the waves and not be as effective. The key is as organic as possible, meaning no rings, bracelets, necklaces, anklets, bras with wires, shoes, hair clips, no metal interference.

What about jeans? I'm not about to strip down in the middle of nowhere to enter a vortex?

Ha Ha, Lisa, but if you must, you can wear jeans.

Message from God

Jesus died (sacrificed) himself so that we could have free choice. Without free choice, there would only be hate. Hate because of not being able to make choices or learn from bad choices. Jesus could have beaten Satan, but by being killed, Satan would still have won because freedom of choice would have been taken away. We have a destiny hand, and a will hand.

The power of choice is what gives us experience and allows us to detour from our path once in a while to live freely. Knowing or understanding this is better than thinking he just sacrificed himself for our sins, even though sin is also a product of free will.